MERLIN REBORN

A DRAGON-MYTH CYCLE PREQUEL

JOSEPH FINLEY

TARASTONE PRESS

ALSO BY JOSEPH FINLEY

The Dragon-Myth Cycle

Enoch's Device

The Key to the Abyss

The Cauldron of God

Dragon-Myth Prequels

Hela's Bane

The Fae Dealings

The Sorceress of Avalon

Merlin Reborn

Other Tales

Mava's Echo: A Short Story of Celtic Myth and Magic

PART ONE
AVALON

CHAPTER I
AWAKENING

It feels like a dream. She stands on a small marsh island in a lake whose waters glow pale, the color of a full moon.

The light bathes the burial mound where he lies.

He is handsome. Stately. A lord in gray robes. A silver beard covers his square jaw, well-groomed like the mustache beneath his sharp nose. Fine lines crease the corners of his eyes, the mark of a wise man.

His eyes flutter open. His irises burn like hot amber.

He opens his mouth and draws in a breath. His first breath in centuries.

She wavers, staring down at him, her head light as air. A fog seeps into her mind. Her left arm hangs numb, but her shoulder screams with pain.

The petrified reed that had pierced her shoulder missed her heart. If not, she would be dead. It missed her lung, for she could still breathe. But she is losing blood.

So much blood.

The man on the burial mound begins to fade. The fog in her mind darkens.

Her world upends, and she is falling.

~

Bradamante opened her eyes. The pain in her shoulder was gone, replaced by a tingling sensation. She flexed her fingers. Warmth prickled through her left arm.

The man gazing down at her held the crystal, blazing white with his soul's light. His fingers, slick with her blood, curled around its glow. He must have found it just where she had left it: tucked beneath his hands, clasped against his chest. And he had used it to heal her. But if it was compassion that moved him, none showed in his cold, unreadable face.

As the light faded from his crystal, he spoke. His words were foreign.

She shook her head.

Frustration creased his brow. "Do you speak Latin?"

She nodded.

"Good," he growled. "Now that you're awake, tell me who you are."

"I saved you," she said, her voice barely a whisper.

"And I returned that favor. So who are you? Did Morgain send you?"

Bradamante grimaced as she pushed herself up on the rocky ground. Her muscles ached, and her chainmail tunic felt heavy on her shoulders. She drew in a breath. "My name is Bradamante, and no, Morgain did not send me."

His amber eyes narrowed as if he were searching for the truth inside her. "Orionde, then?"

"I came here with Orionde's apprentice."

She craned her neck, staring across the lake. The colossal tree loomed like a petrified oak, its highest branches swallowed by Avalon's gloom. Halfway up, a vast, glistening web stretched between its limbs. A dark silhouette hung in its center, barely visible in the glow from the lake.

She pointed. "The witch has him trapped there."

"Witch?" The man, who had to be Merlin, hesitated at the word. "You mean Nimue?"

She gave him another nod. "Your Lady of the Lake has gone mad. And if we linger, I've no doubt she'll put you right back where I found you."

This time, Merlin nodded but made no move to leave. "You don't speak our language. So, where are you from?"

"Francia," she replied, rising to her feet.

His eyes flared with anger. "Orionde enlisted the aid of the Franks? Arthur won't like that. He spent his youth fighting the Franks."

He doesn't know, she realized. *How could he?*

"Arthur is gone." Her words hung in the air. "He died more than two hundred years ago."

Merlin's eyes widened, the color draining from his face. For a heartbeat, his mouth hung open, speechless. Then, he muttered, "What of Britain?"

"It belongs to the Saxons now."

Merlin exhaled a shuddering breath and turned away. "Then all is lost."

"Like hell it is!" she snapped, heat rising up her neck. "I saved you for a reason."

Merlin turned on her, his amber eyes burning. "I am no one's pawn. And you have no idea how much has been lost!"

Bradamante balled her hands into fists.

Then she heard it: a hard, wet slapping against the rocky shore.

Merlin cast a sidelong glance, his anger vanishing into alarm.

She turned sharply, her breath catching in her throat.

Bone-white claws, larger than her hands, dug into the gray rocky shore. A skull-like head lifted from the glowing water, its pale leathery skin hanging in tattered scraps. Red orbs of light simmered in its hollow eye sockets, and a hiss escaped its long snout, revealing a mouthful of jagged teeth longer than her fingers.

Merlin shot her a look, his eyes wide.

"Run!" he said.

CHAPTER 2
LABYRINTH

Roland did not know how many hours he and Turpin had been lost in the maze-like tunnels of Avalon. Every passageway looked the same: endless gloom, rock walls, and patches of green and yellow lichen that gave off a faint glow.

Turpin had been marking their path, striking crosses into the stone with his flanged mace. He claimed his inspiration from the Greek hero Theseus, who had once wandered through a labyrinth ages ago. Roland had always admired the broad-shouldered archbishop's prowess in battle, for there was no finer warrior among the clerics of Francia. But just this once, he found himself grateful for Turpin's love of books and history.

Marking their path had kept them from wandering in circles, most of the time. Yet when another passage led back to a familiar cross, Roland swore under his breath.

"Well, we know not to take that fork again," Turpin sighed.

Roland rubbed his aching forehead. He blamed the

pain as much on this cursed maze as on the emptiness gnawing at his belly.

"It's not as if we have another option," he muttered.

"True."

Turpin led them down the other fork, and Roland followed into yet more gloom. The walls pressed close, the same glowing lichen winking at them from the dark. Roland cursed again.

The more he thought about it, the more he felt their entire mission had been cursed from the start, long before they set foot in Avalon. Their supposedly secret voyage had been uncovered almost at once by some shadowy enemy calling himself the Blackbird. First, it was two of his henchmen, waiting to waylay Maugis before he ever reached the boat. Then, he, or whatever sorcerer was working for them, sent the two demons that followed them to Saint-Julian's. And if that were not enough, a shipload of mercenaries had struck the moment they landed on Britannia's shore. The survivors had warned them that the Blackbird himself was coming to the island, but that was the least of their troubles.

Nimue, the Lady of Avalon, was the real problem.

Twenty of the Blackbird's well-armed mercenaries had been no match for four of Charles's paladins. But Nimue had shattered their company and their mission in seconds. Now Maugis was gone, captured or worse. Bradamante was lost. And he and Turpin were wandering like blind men through these cursed tunnels, hunted by at least one of Nimue's pale, hairless hounds.

As for what else could go wrong, Roland did not even want to think about that.

His stomach rumbled again.

"Don't these Fae ever eat?" he griped. "It would be nice to find a well-stocked kitchen down here."

Turpin stopped and scratched his thick gray beard. "I never thought about that. Do rogue angels need to eat? I'm fairly certain scripture is silent on that point."

Roland managed a faint smile, then noticed the archbishop's shoulder was no longer bleeding through his chainmail. At least that was something.

They reached another fork, and Turpin hammered a cross into the rock.

"Which way this time?" he asked.

Roland started to sigh, then froze. Faint voices echoed from the passage on the right. One voice rose above the others. A woman's. Strained and in trouble.

Roland's breath hitched. *Bradamante!*

"That one," he said, already moving. His hand flew to Durendal's hilt, and the blade rasped free as he charged down the right fork.

CHAPTER 3
THE LETHE DRAKE

Bradamante ran.

Despite Merlin's healing arts, her legs still felt weak. Gritting her teeth, she vaulted two yards over the glowing water onto the nearest island. She stumbled on landing, catching herself on the hard gray rocks. Pain flared in her palms, a fresh reminder of the cuts from the razor-sharp reeds jutting in clusters along the marshlike isles.

She glanced back. Merlin stood on the isle that had been his tomb, facing the horror that had dragged itself onto shore.

The skeletal creature's body was larger than a boar, with a long, bony tail. Its skull, hissing like wind through hollow bones, rocked on a serpentine neck, as if a wingless dragon from the myths of old had emerged from the depths of the lake.

Merlin shouted a word: *"Eoh!"*

A searing beam of white light burst from the crystal in his right hand. The light struck the abomination in the face, and its head whipped back and forth as if Merlin's soul light was more than this unholy creature could bear.

Merlin whirled and leaped from the island. He landed beside her with an agility that belied the fact that he had been asleep for centuries under Nimue's curse.

"Move!" he urged. "I've only stunned it."

Her heart pounded. "What is it?"

"A Lethe drake, long dead. But she's turned it into one of her guardians."

He grabbed her hand and pulled her toward the next isle, only a yard away. He let her leap first, then landed behind her, his boots crunching on the rocks. Ahead, seven small marsh isles dotted the path to the shore that led back into Avalon's labyrinthine tunnels.

As soon as they made the yard-long jump to the next isle, they heard the drake scrabbling across the islands behind them. She glanced back. The drake sprang toward another isle, its claws raking the air, its eyes burning like coals.

She hurled herself across the watery gap to the isle where she'd slain Nimue's first guardian. Its skeletal remains lay in a heap, little more than a pile of bones next to the shards of her shattered longsword.

Merlin sprinted past her, weaving between the spear-like reeds, before jumping. She pushed herself forward behind him, leaping the two-yard gap onto the next island. A heartbeat later, the drake landed where they had just been, its hiss deepening into a growl.

Grimacing, Merlin turned toward the drake, his crystal pinched between his fingers. *"Eoh!"* A searing blast of soul light lanced from the crystal into the creature's skull, causing it to shriek and rear back on its short hind legs.

"Go!" he cried.

Without looking back, she darted toward the next

island. She hopped to the next one, then again, faster this time. Two more leaps, and she reached the patch of land before the tunnel's mouth.

Merlin followed behind, but by the time he reached the shore, the drake was already vaulting across the small isles, thrashing its tail and hissing from open jaws.

Sweat dampened Bradamante's forehead as she hurried into the tunnel. *Keep to the left*, she reminded herself when she encountered the first fork in the twisting passages.

"You know the way?" Merlin asked, huffing behind her.

"It's how I found you."

She reached the chamber first, a roughly round, domed cavern covered in soot and ash. The pale lake's light filtered through three narrow crevices in the rock, casting eerie beams over the scorched remains of what had once been a library.

When Merlin arrived, he stopped suddenly and gasped. "My books …" His hands flew to his temples, and he took a shuddering breath.

"What has she done?" he muttered, barely above a whisper.

"No time to worry about that!" Bradamante said, pulling him into the chamber. From the tunnel, she could hear the drake's claws scraping across the rock.

Merlin shook himself, snapping out of his daze. He rushed to a stone table sitting on a rectangular slab, resembling an altar. "Help me move it," he commanded, already pushing on the heavy tabletop.

She threw her weight against it, shoving it a quarter of the way to reveal a hollow space filled with shadow. Merlin reached in and pulled out a leaf-shaped sword, similar to the one Maugis wielded.

She stepped back, already feeling the thrum in the air that came with the use of Fae power.

Merlin murmured an alien incantation, tracing the air with the blade. As soon as the drake reached the chamber, he shouted another word, and a fierce wind erupted out of nowhere, sweeping up the ash and debris into a howling storm. The black cloud blasted into the undead creature.

The drake roared, its skeletal form blackened with soot. The glow of its ember-like eyes flickered dimly through the swirling ash.

"Do you have an enchanted weapon, by chance?" Merlin asked.

"Of course not," she said sharply. Other than the dagger sheathed in her belt, she didn't have a real weapon at all, at least not one that would do anything to this creature.

"That's unfortunate." He held his crystal now in his left hand and, with a word, sent another beam of soul light searing into the drake's skull.

"I can't stop it," he admitted. "We'll have to flee again!"

She turned to bolt from the chamber when a new roar exploded from the tunnel.

A battle cry!

Two men charged into the chamber, and Bradamante could hardly believe her eyes. There stood her cousin Roland, clad in his chainmail armor, gripping his longsword Durendal. Beside him loomed Archbishop Turpin, brandishing his silver cross like an exorcist.

The drake hissed furiously at Turpin, then turned to Roland as he bore in on the creature. Its jaws snapped at the sleeve of his mail, but Roland flew past them. He hammered Durendal into the drake's neck. Bone shattered. The light in the drake's eye sockets winked away as its massive skull smashed onto the rock-hard ground. Then its entire body collapsed into a pile of bones.

Roland stood over the creature's remains, triumph flashing in his eyes. Then he turned to Bradamante. "Are you hurt, cousin?"

"No," she said.

She glanced at Merlin, who was staring at Roland as if he had seen a ghost. A name tumbled from the wizard's lips.

"Lancelot?"

CHAPTER 4

ECHOES FROM THE PAST

Roland blinked when he heard the name. *Lancelot.* Had Brother Meical mentioned that name before?

The silver-haired stranger stood wide-eyed, staring at Turpin.

"Cadoc?"

Turpin tilted his head as if trying to make sense of the man's words.

Roland stepped forward. *Enough of this.* He spoke in Latin, hoping the stranger would understand him. "My name is Roland, old man, and this is Turpin, Archbishop of Reims. Who in hell are you?"

A confused expression spread across the man's face.

"He is Merlin," Bradamante said. "Everything Brother Meical told us about him was true. Nimue's curse imprisoned him, but I found a way to break the spell."

Merlin.

Now that was a name Roland recognized from Brother Meical's tales. And now that he noticed, the man held a leaf-shaped blade limply in his right hand, the same kind of sword Maugis wielded with his magic to command the wind. Brother Meical had told them Merlin studied with the Fae of Avalon. But if all this were true, this man should be hundreds of years old. It didn't seem possible. Then again, neither did the dragon-like monster he had just slain. Or the fact that they were standing in the Otherworld.

Possible, not possible. What did it matter anymore?

The sword slipped from Merlin's fingers and clattered onto the stone floor. He ran a hand over his face as if trying to wake from a dream.

"You might as well be his twin," Merlin said to Roland before looking at Turpin. "You, as well. Neither of you looks a day older than when we last sat at the Round Table. Yet if Arthur's been gone for hundreds of years, both of you should be … dead."

Roland shook his head and sheathed his sword, unsure what to say to the man, who was clearly confused. But Turpin stepped forward.

"You've mistaken us," Turpin said. "Perhaps there's a reason for that."

"A reason?" Merlin asked.

Roland shrugged, spreading his hands as he exchanged glances with his companions. *What are we doing with this old fool?* he wanted to ask them.

If only the old fool weren't standing right there.

Merlin shook his head. "No … it can't be. Can it?"

As he bent down to pick up his leaf-shaped sword, Roland's fingers wrapped around Durendal's hilt, but Turpin raised a hand to ward him off. "Wait," he whispered.

Turning his back to them, Merlin stared at the curved, soot-stained wall behind the stone table. Where patches of soot had been cleared, Roland noticed writing carved into the wall, mostly in a language he could not read.

Then, he noticed the soot-blackened sleeves of Bradamante's tunic.

She's been here before.

Merlin began moving the sword in a circular motion before muttering those strange Fae words that Maugis did when he worked his magic. An eldritch blue light flickered across the chamber's domed ceiling as a cold wind stirred from nowhere. Roland stepped back as the breeze began to howl before Merlin jerked his sword toward the wall. A gust of wind blasted the soot into a black cloud, which settled on the floor, revealing a ten-foot patch of wall scrawled with more writing.

Merlin set down his sword and walked to the wall. "I used to call this my chamber of visions," he said, tracing the words with his forefinger. "It is where I would lie when the prophecies would come to me in my dream sleep. When I'd awake, I'd carve them into this wall, so they would not be forgotten …"

His fingers focused on a verse scrawled in some Breton tongue.

"Before she imprisoned me …" His voice was distant, as if reliving the moment. "I had one last vision. I called it the prophecy of the Once and Future King."

Turpin raised an eyebrow. "What did you see?"

"I foresaw a king," Merlin said, "so much like Arthur that it could have been him reborn. He was not in Camelot, but in a palace I had never seen, hung with banners bearing golden flowers, like the tips of spears, on a field of blue. And in war, I saw his horsemen ride with a long red standard emblazoned with a golden sun."

Bradamante's eyes went wide, and Roland knew they were thinking the same thing. *Those are the Oriflamme and the fleur-de-lis.*

"This future king," Merlin continued, "would forge a

vast kingdom and defend it against a horde of enemies, both foreign and within his borders. Twelve lords served by his side. Yet in my vision, they were the same lords of war who sat around Arthur's round table. Lancelot and Cadoc, Gawain and Perceval, Kay, Palamedes, Bors, and the others."

Merlin's gaze lifted. "And now, I see the two of you standing in my chamber."

Turpin's eyes lit up, a look Roland had seen before when something became clear in the archbishop's mind.

"We know this king," Turpin said. "His name is Charles, and his kingdom lies across the channel. Some already call him Charles the Great, and we are three of his twelve lords. Roland, here, is chief among them."

Merlin raised an eyebrow. "As was Lancelot, until the betrayal …"

Roland narrowed his gaze. He did not know this Lancelot, but he knew he would never betray Charles.

Though once, I had. Only not by my own will …

"Charles did not send us," Bradamante interjected, "Orionde did. She sent us to retrieve a weapon, one you are familiar with. A weapon whose purpose reaches far beyond Britannia or Francia or any kingdom of this world. But to do this, we need your help."

Merlin's brow furrowed, and a wary look filled his eyes. "You want to steal the weapon from Nimue?"

"Our cause may be the very reason for your vision," Turpin told him. "Orionde serves a power greater than herself, and I see a purpose in your prophecy. Now fate has given you the power to help fulfill it."

Merlin shook his head. "No, this cannot be my destiny. In my vision, I was not among the twelve. The king had another counselor. Similar to me, but it was not me."

To Roland's surprise, Bradamante seized Merlin by the

sleeve of his gray robes and pulled him toward the window-like crevices. The old man let out a grunt of protest but didn't pull away. His skin looked pale in the light shining through the gaps.

Roland followed, catching his first glimpse of the luminescent lake through the narrow crevices in the rock wall. The colossal tree rose from the waters like a mountain. Between its branches stretched strands that shimmered like the web of some enormous spider. Something was ensnared in the web's center. Roland squinted, a chill creeping up his neck.

Is that a man?

Bradamante thrust her arm through one of the crevices, pointing at the tree. Then she turned to Merlin, locking eyes with him.

"The king's counselor is named Maugis," she said, her voice like steel. "Nimue has him trapped there, and you're going to help me save him."

CHAPTER 5

THE SPIDER'S WEB

Maugis gasped for breath. He hung there in the enormous web, his limbs splayed and wrapped tightly in hundreds of silky strands that formed the web.

The Lethe spiders, glossy white creatures larger than his hands, scurried across his chest and down his limbs, occasionally applying slick new strands of webbing from the tips of their diamond-shaped abdomens. They stared at him with an array of black eyes, their mandibles clicking and clacking as if eager to feast on their prey.

His head throbbed from the waning effects of Nimue's elixir, leaving him feeling as if he had drunk too much wine. Her potion had stolen his will to resist and loosened his tongue so that he told her everything she wanted to know, ripping open old wounds deep inside him that had never healed. She had gone to retrieve more elixir, leaving the stone terrace carved into the titanic, petrified tree like a parapet, empty save for the stool on which she sat when listening to his tales.

A cold dread settled in his chest. He did not want to

finish the story. He knew how it ended, and that ending was too painful to bear. But she would make him tell it, and in his current condition, how could he stop her?

Hinges screamed as the iron-bound door, carved into the trunk of the massive tree, slowly opened. Maugis sucked in a breath as Nimue emerged from its shadows, tall and barefoot, her figure wrapped in a long gossamer dress that clung to her hips and breasts. Silver hair cascaded over her shoulders, framing an ageless face, beautiful yet cold, like frost on steel. In antiquity, the Fae had been viewed as gods, and Maugis imagined she could have been Isis or Hecate, a goddess of passion and darkness.

Between her fingers, the crystal vial of elixir gleamed with a violet hue. The memory of that liquid burning down his throat churned his stomach, but it was the knowledge of what would come next that twisted like a knife in his gut.

"So," she asked, "where were we? Morgain and her miraculous daughter Angelica burned Orionde's library to ashes and then stole away from Rosefleur. I imagine they took the *Book of Shadows* with them. That can't be good."

Maugis grimaced, his voice hoarse and ragged. "No."

"You know that book cannot be destroyed," she said. "You could set one of its pages on fire, and the vellum simply absorbs the flames. You could store it at the bottom of a well, but the water wouldn't even cause the ink to run. We had the mightiest warrior in Atlantis strike it with an axe, and the iron blade shattered before even a scratch appeared on its cover. Some believe the book is a part of its author, Astaroth, and as long as he exists, so will the book. But of course, Astaroth is one of the nine sons of the Dragon himself, and who knows if a demon that powerful could ever be killed?"

Astaroth ...

Maugis fought back the urge to retch upon hearing the name. It was a name he had hoped to banish from his thoughts, but the memory of what the demon had done lingered like a nightmare in the back of his mind.

Nimue stepped closer until she was mere feet from where he hung in the gigantic web. "You know where Morgain and Angelica went, don't you?"

Maugis lifted his head, then nodded.

"And you know what happened to them. You know where they are now."

He let out a shuddering sigh. "Don't make me go there."

"Make you?" She reached up and seized his chin so hard it felt as if she could break his jaw with a clench of her fingers. She pulled his mouth open and poured in the vial's contents. The liquid seared down his throat and into his stomach before sending a wave of heat through his veins.

"You'll go there willingly," she said. "You'll tell me everything I want to know."

His head was already feeling light. Any hope of resisting her began bleeding away until all he could focus on was the sound of her voice. Such a beautiful, intoxicating voice.

She stroked his cheek and brushed his lips with her fingertips. "Now tell me, how did you find them again?"

Maugis could only do what she asked.

"It began," he murmured, "with a war ... and whispers of a witch."

PART TWO
VERONA

CHAPTER 6

THE WINDS OF WAR

The war began with a death that would change the fate of Francia.

At the time, my king, Charles, ruled half of his late father's kingdom, while his younger brother, Carloman, controlled the rest. Charles owned all the land in the north and along the western coast, while Carloman's domain included Paris, Reims, Burgundy, and most of Germania. He also ruled half of Aquitaine, Cognac, Provence, and all the land bordering the kingdom of Lombardy. It was a considerable inheritance. And it was the only thing keeping Charles from ruling all of Francia.

For months, Charles and Carloman had been on the edge of outright war, and I feared the blood of thousands might be spilled over their rivalry. But then, in December of 771, fate saved the kingdom from civil war when Carloman fell ill and passed away overnight. He was only twenty years old. He left behind his young wife, Gerberga, and two sons, the eldest no older than three.

They were the problem.

You see, those boys held claim to their father's vast

kingdom, and while I never would have imagined Charles harming them, their mother feared otherwise. She fled with her sons to Lombardy, where she was welcomed by the Lombard king Desiderius and his son, Prince Adalgis. That was the first spark in a conflict waiting to ignite, and what came next would only feed the flames. For not long after their arrival in Lombardy, King Desiderius declared his support for her sons' claim to their late father's throne.

Desiderius was no friend of Charles. A year earlier, the Lombard king gave his daughter, Desiderata, to Charles in marriage. She was eighteen, quite vain, and utterly spoiled. I never cared for her, and neither did Charles. The union was one of political convenience, but within the year, Charles repudiated the marriage and shipped her home to her father. Charles even had any mention of the nuptials erased from the royal annals. From that day on, the Lombard king viewed Charles as his sworn enemy. But Desiderius had an even greater foe: Hadrian, the new pope in Rome.

The Holy Father viewed the Lombard king as a direct threat to his supremacy. Desiderius's embrace of Carloman's sons and their royal claim gave the pope the opportunity he needed to eliminate that threat. The pope's ambassador set sail for Marseilles to deliver a message to Charles. The letter arrived in a gilded scroll case, and its scented vellum bore the pope's crimson wax seal. It warned that the Lombards planned to conquer Rome and implored Charles, in the name of God and the Prince of the Apostles, to hasten to Lombardy before the pope and his curia were destroyed. I doubt anything the pope wrote in the message was true, but it worked.

For in the spring of 773, Charles raised an army, forty thousand strong, and I rode with him to wage war on Lombardy.

We passed through the Alps and reached the border of Lombardy, where we overwhelmed Desiderius's fortifications. Roland, the Lord Commander of the Breton March, led a smaller force in a flank attack, sending the lion's share of the enemy fleeing to Pavia, the Lombard capital. We encountered little resistance after that and arrived at Pavia to discover that Desiderius and his forces had opted to defend the city from behind its formidable stone walls. Charles ordered a blockade, and we settled in for what promised to be a months-long siege.

What we had not anticipated was that Prince Adalgis, like a fool, had fallen in love. Carloman's pretty young widow, Gerberga, was the object of his affection, and he fled the city with her and her sons before we arrived. Charles's spies soon learned that Gerberga and her lovelorn prince were holed up in Verona along with her two boys. That was the moment Charles's plans changed. He decided to leave the siege of Pavia to his uncle, Bernard, and Ganelon, one of his paladins, while he led ten thousand men to take Verona. I and the rest of his paladins went with him.

Three days into our march, Roland volunteered to lead a scouting expedition. He figured Prince Adalgis would have his scouts on the road, and it would be to our advantage to intercept them. Roland's cousin, Bradamante, was the first to raise her hand to join the expedition. Charles asked me to go, too, along with my own cousins, Renaud and Guichard, and two more of the paladins, Olivier of Vienne and Huon of Bordeaux. With us were thirty chevaliers, all seasoned warriors who were among the finest horsemen in Francia.

It was a perfect day for riding. The day was fair, the sky

a pale blue, and a light breeze stirred the air. We traveled through the woodlands, keeping an eye on the shallow valley, where honey-gold meadows mixed with swaths of lush green grass. I rode Bayard, my massive stallion, whose bay coat was protected by thick leather barding. I wore my own armor, a long-sleeved chainmail hauberk, and carried my iron-rimmed shield, whose leather cover bore the symbol of Aygremont: a golden leopard on a sable field. Over my hauberk, draped my sable cloak, and, like the others, I had pulled my hood over my helmet to prevent the sunlight from gleaming off the polished metal like a warning beacon to our enemies.

An hour after midday, we found our quarry. Olivier, who had eyes like a hawk, spotted them first: twenty mail-clad horsemen moving slowly through the valley. Which meant we outnumbered them by seventeen men.

"Looks like we'll have some fun today after all," said Renaud, riding to my left on his black charger. My cousin's blue eyes gleamed with excitement, and his wavy auburn hair peeked out beneath his helmet, gathering around his neck in the hollow of his hood.

"Alas," quipped Guichard to my right, "it's the cheva-lier's dream to skewer a host of horsemen right after lunch. Although I would have preferred my lunch to have been a hot bowl of rabbit stew served by a couple of wanton tavern maids instead of stale bread." He finished with a broad grin.

"I'd prefer we just get on with it," I muttered. I would have preferred most things over a cavalry charge, but I was a chevalier, and duty was calling.

Roland led the assault. He burst out of the woods astride his white warhorse, Veillantif, his long spear couched under his right arm. As if sensing the thrill of battle and never wanting to be left out, Bayard charged after Veillantif. In a breath, we were off: thirty-seven cheva-liers thundering downhill into the valley.

At the sight of us, the Lombard scouts wheeled their mounts to flee east toward Verona. We were hundreds of yards behind them, but we were gaining fast due to the momentum of our charge and the Lombards' stunned and delayed reaction. Bayard, the fastest of our horses, surged ahead, forcing me to tug on the reins to keep him from overtaking Veillantif. Behind us roared the pounding of hooves and cries of battle.

"For God and Saint Pierre!" Renaud bellowed.

"For Charles!" the others roared.

As we closed in, the slowest of the fleeing Lombards glanced back, fear in their eyes. Roland was the first to strike, ramming his spear into the back of one of the horsemen. The man shouted in pain before slumping forward in his saddle. Roland ripped the spear free, then drove it into another Lombard's ribs. Before I could blink, Bayard had reached another of the horsemen. The rider twisted in his saddle, raising his sword to bring it down on Bayard's head. But Bayard was too quick. He bit down on the man's arm and yanked him from his saddle, sending him rolling into the wave of incoming horses behind us.

I thrust my spear at another horseman, who knocked it away with his shield just before Renaud rode up on the man's other side and jammed a spear into his armpit. I gave my cousin a grateful nod. A half dozen of the slowest Lombards had fallen, but the rest galloped toward the riverbank, flanked to the right by a thick line of trees. One of the Lombard riders blew two sharp notes on a horn. An instant later, the shadows between the trees stirred, then burst into motion. A host of horsemen cantered out of the treeline, maybe twenty in all. The fleeing Lombards turned their mounts to face us on the riverbank. Roland raised his right hand to slow our charge; somewhere, he had lost his spear. More horsemen were pouring out of the forest, and in an instant, we were the ones outnumbered. I sucked in a breath as I realized what was happening. The Lombard scouts had been lying in wait, baiting us to pursue them. And like overeager fools, we had ridden straight into their trap.

My heart was pounding in my chest from the thrill of the chase, but my stomach clenched tight at the sight of the amassing enemy. Roland slowed us to a stop thirty yards from the enemy line. Bayard snorted and tossed his head, his muscles bunched beneath me, still itching to charge. I pulled hard on the reins and murmured to him, low and firm, until I felt his steps begin to steady.

Along the riverbank, our newly gathered enemy faced us, a host of horsemen clad in mail tunics and round iron helmets, armed like us with round shields, spears, and swords. I was twenty-six at the time, but most of the Lombards looked younger, some just boyish teens. But there were enough veteran-looking warriors, including a few with gray-flecked beards, to remind us that seasoned chevaliers rode with this band. As I finished counting, bile rose in my throat. There were fifty horsemen in all. We were badly outmanned.

One of the Lombards cantered his horse forward. He appeared to be their leader, judging by his hard face and the golden eagle on his shield. "Lord Commander Roland, I've heard of you," he announced with a look of disdain that matched the tone of his voice. "It was foolish for your king, Charles, to invade Lombardy. King Desiderius has enough supplies to outlast your siege of Pavia, and our prince has the walls of Verona fortified with thousands of men. You would be wise to turn around and ride back to your king, where you should advise him to retreat to Francia."

The Lombard's lips curled into a cold smile. "Though, I suppose, sending him your head in a sack would convey the same message."

A few of the men around me muttered curses. Roland did not flinch.

Between Roland and me, Huon trotted forward on his chestnut warhorse. He was a broad-shouldered bear of a man, two years older than me, with a short blond beard and a crooked nose that had been broken last year in battle. He still held his spear, along with his battleaxe strapped to his saddle.

"There's a lot of those bastards," he said to Roland. "What's your plan?"

"The only plan I ever have," Roland muttered before raising his chin and fixing his gaze on the Lombard commander. "Unlike your prince," he shouted, "our King does not shy away from battles, and neither do his lords. You're going to learn that the hard way!"

I drew in a sharp breath at the thought of what would come next, but I was not surprised. Roland had never backed down from a fight, and I knew today would not be his first time. When he slid his sword from his scabbard, Durendal rang like the first note of a battle song.

And then we charged.

CHAPTER 7
WHISPERS OF A WITCH

My first battle on horseback had been six years ago when I faced my brother's army at Brosse. Back then, it was pure chaos, a terrifying clash of horses, steel, and blood. This fight was no less harrowing, no less chaotic. But this time, I had Bayard.

The instant we reached the enemy line, Bayard reared back on his hind legs. Although it exposed his belly beneath the leather barding on his chest, the sight of the massive stallion startled the horseman in front of him. The Lombard's horse let out a fearful whinny as Bayard hammered his right hoof into the horseman's face, smashing his helmet into his skull. Bayard's other hoof kicked his horse's head, sending the animal reeling.

In the now open gap, a younger horseman with a pock-marked face thrust his spear at Renaud, who blocked it with his shield. But the Lombard had exposed his ribs, so I stabbed my spear through his mail and into his side. The wounded horseman twisted in the saddle, his frantic mount spinning away and wrenching my spear from my grasp. Yet Renaud was there with his own spear to finish the man.

Another horseman slashed at Renaud, grazing his mailed shoulder. A heartbeat later, Guichard drove his spear into the man's neck.

I ripped my sword from its scabbard. The short sword, with its leaf-shaped blade, was less than ideal for fighting on horseback. But Bayard was the equalizer. He bit at the enemy riders, tearing another from his mount, before rising up to bring his hoofs down on another man and his horse. Another horseman charged at me. His spear tip scraped against my shield, slicing through the leather cover, but it was stopped by the shield boards. His momentum brought him close enough for me to ram my sword into his neck below the leather chinstrap of his helmet. His blue eyes flew wide as blood pulsed from the wound.

Catching my breath, I glanced to my right. Our flanks would be critical points in this battle, for that's where the Lombard horsemen would try to envelop us. Sure enough, that had already started, and several of our horses were riderless; others were being pressed together, one of our horsemen for every two of theirs.

All around us, the air rang with the clang of steel, the pounding of hooves, the cries of horses, and the cries of men. A blast of pain shuddered up my left arm. I saw a flash of steel as the horseman engaging me brought down his sword again, crashing against my shield. I heard willow boards crack and felt a stab of pain in my wrist. The horseman, face red with anger, bellowed a curse as he stabbed his blade toward my neck. I leaned back, catching the strike on the iron rim of my shield, but the effort nearly tossed me from my saddle. I pressed my thighs against Bayard's ribs to keep from falling. The Lombard hefted his sword for another blow before a battleaxe smashed into his face, nearly cleaving his head in two and splattering me with gore. I blinked blood from my eyes and looked up into Huon's fierce glare.

Huon turned to meet his next attacker. He swung his battleaxe, bellowing with rage. The axe took a man's arm, then buried its blade into his horse's neck. The animal screamed as it collapsed. Beside him, Roland pressed Veillantif into the enemy ranks. Durendal scythed through the air, separating a Lombard's head from his neck. With another strike, the Fae-forged blade sheared through a man's shield. Before the man could react, Roland pulled his blade free and punched it into the man's throat, only to withdraw as fast as a striking serpent and cleave it backhanded into another horseman's jaw. In all my life, I had never seen a more fearsome fighter than Roland, and all around him, men fell.

"Maugis!"

The sound of my name tore my gaze from Roland an instant before a spear blade sped toward my face. I swatted it away with a desperate parry before Renaud, who had called my name, drove his own spear into the man's ribs. Behind him, Guichard grappled with a Lombard. My jaw dropped as both men tumbled from their saddles, crashing to the ground amid a hail of pounding hooves. Fortunately, Renaud was beside them, and he stabbed his spear through the Lombard, allowing Guichard to scramble away. My younger cousin ripped his sword from his scabbard and finished his attacker, who was already reeling from Renaud's spear thrust.

Several of the Lombards began to retreat, wading their horses into the river. But right behind them was Roland, swinging Durendal with lethal precision. These Lombards were capable warriors, but none could match Roland's prowess, and judging by the swath of fallen men around him, he was worth ten of their men, maybe more. Beyond him, Olivier and Bradamante's spears drove more horsemen into the river, while to Roland's right, Huon cleared away enemy riders with merciless blows of his battleaxe.

To my right, several more of our chevaliers had fallen, but Renaud, whose skills were second only to Roland's, had drawn his sword and was harvesting his own crop of dead and wounded Lombards. The moment a man hit the ground, Guichard was there, sword in hand, to finish the job. The Lombards on our right flank were thinning; we no longer risked being surrounded, on that side, at least. Meanwhile, Bayard took the battle to our enemies, smashing heads with his mighty hooves and biting enemy mounts, causing the panicked horses to buck and throw their riders, right into the path of Guichard's waiting blade.

Loud splashing in the river drew my attention there. More than a dozen of the Lombard horsemen were wading to the other side, where a half-dozen more were already fleeing to the east. Roland had stopped his pursuit and was now dragging what looked like the Lombard commander from his saddle. Huon let his bloodstained battleaxe hang at his side, spent. Beyond him, Bradamante and Olivier urged their horses back onto the riverbank.

My heartbeat began to settle as we waited for the last of the Lombards to ride off. By my count, we had lost eleven brave chevaliers, but almost thirty of our enemy lay dead or wounded on the ground beside the bodies of fallen horses. I dismounted and joined Roland and my fellow paladins for the interrogation of the Lombard leader. The man's once-hard face was bruised and swollen on the left side. His helmet was gone, and his light brown hair hung limp, matted with sweat and blood. A red smear darkened his neck, where his right ear had once been.

Roland lifted the man's head off the ground, gripping the collar of his mail. The man's lips and teeth were stained with blood. I guessed he would not live much longer.

"Tell me about Verona's defenses," Roland growled.

The Lombard snarled defiantly. Roland slapped him beside the head where his ear had been, causing the man to yowl in pain.

The Lombard swallowed hard. "The prince has three thousand archers and men-at-arms to man the walls, several hundred more guarding his palace, along with the city's militia. The people of Verona are proud. They say, 'To hell with you, Franks,' and they're willing to fight."

Roland narrowed his eyes. "Is that all?"

The man choked out a laugh, blood dripping from his lips onto his beard. "No, the prince employs a witch." He bared his teeth. "She'll rain curses down on you, poison your water, foul your air, and fill your bellies with worms. You won't have enough carts to take back your sick and your dead by the time she's finished with you."

The man's lips twisted into a blood-stained grin.

Roland released his grip, letting the man's head hit the ground. The Lord Commander rose to his feet and pulled me aside. "What do you think?" he asked under his breath.

I shook my head. "Even if this witch is real, she won't be trained. I doubt she'll know anything of the true power."

"Good," he said, clapping me on the shoulder.

I drew in a confident breath, certain I was right. For that's what I had been taught about women who called themselves witches.

But I could not have been more wrong.

CHAPTER 8
ADALGIS

"A witch?" Charles said, a note of incredulity in his voice.

I had informed him of this development that evening in his tent, a spacious abode of crimson canvas trimmed with gold and well-lit by a collection of oil lamps scented with rosemary. Roland, Renaud, and Guichard joined me, all of us still in our armor, though we had taken steps to clean off much of the blood and grime before presenting ourselves to our king. Turpin, the Archbishop of Reims, was already there, dressed similarly to Charles in a silk-trimmed tunic and a woolen cloak instead of his armor or clerical vestments.

Charles stood beside the archbishop, holding a pewter cup of wine. He was nearly as tall as Turpin and broad across the chest, with arms sculpted by years of swordcraft. His golden blond hair fell to his shoulders, and his beard was flecked lightly with silver. His regal face typically wore a ready smile, but it could vanish in an instant when his legendary temper flared like a birchbark torch. Yet upon hearing our news tonight, his expression was a mix of surprise and amusement.

Charles shook his head. "Has Adalgis lost his ever-loving mind? I would think Bishop Anno and his priests would want to burn this witch at the stake and have Adalgis excommunicated for harboring her."

"Of course he would," Renaud said. "Bishops love nothing more than a good witch-burning."

Roland shrugged. "Why not have Turpin send word to Bishop Anno? If Adalgis has allied himself with some heretic crone, maybe the bishop will unlock the city gates and welcome us with open arms?"

Charles looked to Turpin, who nodded. "It's worth a try," the archbishop admitted.

"Assuming she's some shriveled-up crone," Guichard said with his wry smile. "What if she's young, supple, with long legs, long hair, ample breasts? More like a seductive enchantress than a ghastly crone. Maybe she's averse to clothing, too. For all we know, she might already have Anno under her spell, sharing his bed three times a day. Ah, to have the life of a bishop!"

Turpin shot Guichard a disapproving look, but Charles' lips curled into a smile.

"Maugis," the king asked as a thoughtful expression settled on his face, "what has Orionde told you about witches? Is there any reason we should be concerned?"

"Many witches are mere charlatans," I replied. "There's nothing magical about them. Others might be skilled in herb craft, healers mostly who cling to the pagan ways of old. A rarer few might have access to the power through secrets passed down in their covens over the centuries. But even these know only scraps or fragments of the true mysteries, and they have no formal training in it.

They would pose little danger to anyone who has learned to master the power."

Charles studied me for a moment, then clapped a hand on my shoulder. "Then it's a good thing we have a true master on our side."

Charles's confidence sent a swell of pride through my veins. There were few men I respected more than Charles, and to have his affirmation was worth more to me than a purse filled with gold.

Charles turned back to Turpin. "Send a priest to Bishop Anno, condemning the prince's heresy and asking him to welcome us into Verona. Once we're inside the city walls, this conflict will end swiftly."

"Of course, Your Highness," Turpin replied with a nod. "Let's pray Bishop Anno still remembers who he serves."

"And if he's fallen under this witch's spell?" Guichard asked, still amused with himself.

Charles placed a hand on the pommel of his longsword, Joyeuse. "Then I trust my resourceful paladins will find a way into the city to open the gates. And then we'll settle this the hard way."

BISHOP ANNO DID NOT WELCOME us with open arms.

The priests we had sent with Turpin's letter returned when we were a day's march from Verona. They carried Anno's reply, penned on fine vellum and sealed with scarlet wax. The bishop expressed his sincere displeasure at Charles's invasion of Lombardy and the siege of Pavia while affirming his steadfast loyalty to King Desiderius, Prince Adalgis, and the kingdom of Lombardy. The letter said nothing of the pope's role in this conflict and not a word about Adalgis's witch or the allegations of heresy that Turpin had emphasized in his own letter. Instead, he requested a parlay under a white banner, where he and the prince hoped to negotiate a swift and bloodless resolution to the standoff.

Charles's temper flared as Turpin read the letter aloud, but the fire passed quickly. He grew quiet, his jaw tight with resolve. Adalgis may have been a prince and older by a year, but Charles had never regarded his former brother-in-law as an equal.

The next day, our army arrived at Verona. Turpin's priests had warned us about the city's daunting fortifications, and they had not been wrong. The outer walls rose more than thirty feet high, built of ancient Roman stone patched with Lombard brick, and were guarded every sixty yards by square towers crowned with battlements. Beyond them, the priests claimed, stood a second ring of walls, relics of an earlier Roman age, but no less formidable. And past that second wall, in the city's heart, loomed the prince's fortress-like palace.

The river Adige curved around the city's western, northern, and eastern flanks, leaving the southern wall and its main gate as our only way forward. Red and gold banners fluttered above the towers while Lombard archers moved behind the crenellations like ants upon a hill. Where the old Roman road ended, a massive gatehouse rose, with four stone towers bristling with bowmen. The wooden gates beneath it were shut tight, sealed behind an arch of red Lombard brick and white Roman stone. The only way into Verona would be through those gates or over those walls, and we would have to weather a storm of arrows to reach either one.

We established camp a third of a mile from the city, far out of bowshot but close enough to keep a vigilant watch on the walls. Men dug a long trench at the camp's edge while others raised tents for the men-at-arms, followed by pens for the horses. A makeshift smithy went up beside the pens, and beyond it stood tents for our archers and cavalry. Charles's crimson pavilion was pitched behind them, at the center of the camp, beside Turpin's. I shared a tent with my cousins, Renaud and Guichard, just behind the king's and adjacent to the one shared by Roland and Olivier. Around us, the rest of Charles's paladins and high nobles clustered their tents like a village forming around a lord's hall. Beyond that spread the support quarters: tents for servants, smiths, cooks, and clergy, along with the long line of supply wagons that had groaned behind us all the way from Pavia.

I slept restlessly that night, though I could not say exactly why. I had no reason to fear this witch, but something about Bishop Anno's continued loyalty to the prince unsettled me. In the morning, I donned my armor and sable cloak and joined Charles to prepare for the parlay. The bishop's invitation had called for six envoys from each side, and Charles chose carefully. Archbishop Turpin would accompany him, as would I, in my role as royal counselor. With us rode Roland, Lord Commander of the Breton March; Renaud, heir to the Duchy of Dordogne; and Naimon, Duke of Bavaria. All of us wore our finest mail, polished to a silver shine, including Turpin, who bore a golden cross over his chest, a clear sign that he was as much a warrior as a cleric.

I gripped Bayard's reins tightly as we trotted toward the meeting ground, a stretch of open field three hundred yards from the city gates. Six riders emerged one by one from the towering archway, the lead horseman bearing a white banner that swayed gently in the morning breeze. As our parties drew closer, I spotted Adalgis riding behind the strong-jawed chevalier carrying the prince's banner. My first thought was that Adalgis fancied himself as King Midas from the old Greek tales. His mail shone with gleaming gold, and even the barding on his roan stallion held a golden hue. His reddish-blond curls framed his plump cheeks and upturned nose, then gathered at his neck around a high golden collar that curved behind his head like an absurd halo. His cheeks were flushed pink, and his piggishly small eyes added to his perpetually haughty expression.

"He looks like a fat, gilded peacock," Renaud said, leaning toward me in his saddle.

I laughed aloud, but the humor dissipated when I noticed the riders behind Adalgis. One, dressed in a bishop's black cassock and skull cap, was Bishop Anno. A short silver beard framed his jaw, and the skin beneath was ruddy and puffy, as if the man were too fond of wine. Two more chevaliers rode behind the bishop, decked in mail and helmets adorned with the long plumes of horsehair that the Lombards admired. But it was the hooded figure beside the bishop, riding a black mare, that caught my attention. The slight form indicated it was a woman, though she was draped in black robes and sat stooped in her saddle, causing her face to be lost in the shadow of a deep cowl.

So, Adalgis had brought his witch, and she's riding alongside the bishop, too.

We slowed our horses to a stop ten yards from the prince's party. Charles spoke first. "Adalgis," he said with a hint of contempt, "I trust you've summoned us here to spare your people the cost of further bloodshed."

Adalgis stifled a laugh, then raised his right hand sheathed in a golden glove. "Charles," he said in his high-pitched voice with an almost dramatic sigh. "When you so callously sent my sister back from your wedding bed, I had thought you'd stay away from Lombardy." He swept his hand toward us with a theatrical flourish. "Yet here you are."

Charles set his jaw, a flicker of anger rising behind his gaze. "I am here. Along with ten thousand men, and among them, the finest warriors in Francia. You are outnumbered, Adalgis. And there will be no reinforcements from your father in Pavia. You know that. Pavia will fall, and the Kingdom of Lombardy will be mine."

Adalgis's eyes narrowed into a glare as a red hue filled his cheeks. "Such ambition," he sneered. "It's rotted your sense of kinship. The moment your brother died, you moved against his widow—your own sister-in-law—and tried to steal his kingdom from his sons." His lips curled, and his voice rose with fury. "I promise you this: Gerberga and her sons will come to no harm. And one day, they shall reclaim their father's kingdom. The world will know you not as emperor, but as a half-king, half a man, twisted by your vile ambition."

Charles's grip tightened on his stallion's reins, his muscles twitching. Turpin reached out and gently touched the king's arm. With a look, the archbishop made his plea: *Let me speak.*

"Bishop Anno," Turpin said, "I wrote to you of grave allegations concerning heresy in His Highness, the prince. You did not bother even to acknowledge those concerns in your letter, and now I find you by his side, next to this one." He pointed to the cowled woman on the black mare. "Did you come here today with the prince's witch?"

Anno's face went pale. He turned his head, unable to look Turpin in the eyes.

But Adalgis scoffed. "She is no witch. She is a holy woman." He uttered those words with reverence. "She speaks with the angels, and they have revealed to her many great things. Why, it was they who informed her of your coming to Verona so we would be prepared. And through them, she has foreseen the fate that awaits you if you do not leave Lombardy with haste. Your camp shall be visited by plague, and sickness and death will run rampant among your men. Your companions will turn on one another, and the bloodshed on both sides within your ranks shall be your own. Once it is done, your famous paladins will be no more, and you will leave here broken. A king whose peers are buried underground. And hence, there will be no one to aid you when Carloman's sons come to reclaim their father's stolen throne."

Charles swore under his breath. "We will not be frightened by the words of some shriveled crone."

"A shriveled crone?" A coy smile formed on Adalgis's lips. "Show them, my dear."

The woman astride the mare lifted pale, slender hands to her cowl and drew it back.

Beside me, Renaud let out a gasp.

The morning light reflected off her long, raven-black hair, framing a delicate face with bright green eyes I had seen a hundred times in my memory.

Angelica.

My breath caught in my throat. The sight of her after four long years struck like a hammer to the chest. I felt as if the earth had tilted beneath Bayard's hooves. My limbs went cold. After everything that happened on that cursed day at Rosefleur, I thought I would never see her again. And yet here she was. My Angelica. My first love. My only love. My equal in all things, especially in the arts of the Fae. And now, she rode as my enemy.

I barely remember how the parlay ended, so fixed was I on the woman I had known so intimately.

Angelica. How could it be?

The spell broke only when Charles abruptly turned his horse and ended the negotiation. The look he gave me was hard and heavy with displeasure. Around us, Renaud and Roland wore expressions of shock and confusion. They had both fancied Angelica from our long days at court together. But they could not have felt what I felt.

A sword to the gut would have been kinder.

As our party neared our camp, Charles leaned toward me in the saddle.

"We need to talk," he said in a voice as sharp as steel.

CHAPTER 9

A HARD OATH

Charles flung open the flap to his tent and stormed inside.

I hurried after him, with Turpin, Renaud, and Roland close behind. Once inside, Charles turned on me, his face red with anger. "What in the bloody hell is she doing here?"

I winced at his tone. "I do not know, my lord. I haven't seen her for four years."

Charles's eyes narrowed. "But she's no witch." He paused. "She's like you, isn't she?"

"Yes," I admitted, "she was Orionde's apprentice long before I set foot in Rosefleur."

That was all I told him. But I left out the truth: Angelica was nothing like me at all. She was only half human. Her mother, Morgain, was one of the Fae. What that made her, even Orionde could not say. But I had little doubt she was more powerful than I ever would be. And yet, I did not fear her. I longed for her. For the woman she once was. For the lover I had lost. Seeing her now, arrayed as my enemy, twisted like a knife in my heart.

Roland stared at me, arms crossed. Renaud still looked stunned. Turpin scratched his beard, concern etched into every line of his face.

Charles let out a frustrated sigh. "Is she capable of doing the things Adalgis threatened she could do?"

I swallowed hard. "I don't know."

"What do you mean you don't know?" Roland pressed.

"I don't know, damn it!" I snapped. "That's not how the power works. I couldn't summon a plague any more than I could fly to the moon. But back at Rosefleur, she found a book. It was a grimoire called the *Book of Shadows*. Its author was a demon. Its pages held dark, forbidden magics. Secrets unlike anything Orionde ever taught us."

"My God," Turpin muttered under his breath. "Does she still have this book?"

"She took it with her when she left Rosefleur," I said. "That was after the last time I saw her. Orionde warned me that the book corrupts whoever reads it. If Angelica has had that book for four years, I can only imagine what it might have done to her by now."

"So we *are* at risk," Charles said with a grimace.

"Far more than I had anticipated," I admitted.

"Yet, what does that really change?" Roland asked, holding out his palms. "This war will be won with swords and arrows, and we have more of them than Adalgis. He still has his walls, but we'll breach them, as we always do. And if Angelica is now his sorceress, we still have Maugis."

"And," Turpin added, "if she's in league with demons, then we have God and the saints on our side, too."

Their words lifted my spirits, but only slightly. I knew I owed my king more than just hope.

I looked Charles in the eyes. "If Angelica moves against us, my lord, I swear I'll do everything in my power to stop her."

He regarded me for a long moment, as if weighing my words. "Even if it means you have to kill her?" he finally asked.

A cold pain settled in my chest. I didn't want to answer. But I had sworn my oath.

I forced the words past the knot in my throat. "Yes, my lord."

CHAPTER 10

THE SORCERESS
OF VERONA

By the afternoon, the camp was as busy as a village on harvest day. Men were dragging felled trees from the nearby woods and using them to make ladders to scale the walls, while those with the thickest trunks were being fashioned into battering rams. Others bundled the remaining branches to use as firewood for the hundreds of cookfires and watchfires that would soon be blazing throughout the camp. A tang of woodsmoke from fires already burning mixed with the scents of hay and horse sweat. Along the river, scouts patrolled the banks and bridges to prevent any boats from reaching the city. In the ditch in front of the camp, scores of men were hammering sharpened stakes, while others erected timber watch towers to monitor the city walls.

I rode Bayard to where the watch towers were being constructed and peered at the city's walls, hoping to catch a glimpse of Angelica. Fading sunlight glinted off the iron helmets of a hundred archers posted along the parapets of those forbidding walls. The top of the hulking gatehouse was even thicker with men, but among them, I spotted a slender figure dressed in black.

My heart skipped a beat. Even before I recognized the way she moved, I felt it was her. Had she been looking for me, as well?

I felt inexplicably drawn to her, as if she had unleashed some spell of summoning. But I knew this was not magic. There was no sizzle on the breeze or thrum in the air. No, this was love and pain. Agony over what had happened between us and longing to see her again. Before I realized it, I was guiding Bayard toward the gatehouse.

"Lord!" men cried out behind me. "What are you doing? There are archers on that wall!"

I ignored them, though my heart began drumming in my chest. As I cantered Bayard into bow range, I knew at any moment that a shaft could pierce my heart. Had I been thinking rationally, I would have known this was foolish beyond reason. Yet, when I saw the black-clad figure raise her arms and heard her shouts carrying from the walls, I pressed on. She would not let them harm me, and that thought kindled a spark of hope.

Did she feel this longing, too?

No one stopped me. I rode until I was twenty yards from the gatehouse, its battlements looming more than forty feet above me. Red banners emblazoned with Desiderius's golden eagle draped from the parapets, rustling gently in the breeze. More than a score of archers stood behind those parapets with arrows knocked on bowstrings. Before I could take a breath, any one of them could have ended my life. But she would not let that happen.

Angelica stood among the archers, gazing down at me, her long raven hair spilling over the black cloak that covered her shoulders. Even from that distance, I could see the green in her eyes and the red gleam of her lips. A tingle of warmth filled my chest, and I sucked in a breath. But then I noticed the leather book satchel hanging from her left shoulder, and I had no doubt what was inside it. A cold dread slid through my veins.

Atop the battlement, the hint of a smile formed on her lips. With a casual shrug, she let her cloak slough away from her right shoulder, revealing her bare, slender arm. Arcane symbols, the color of dried blood, covered her skin. Those symbols, tattooed forever into her flesh, were the price she had paid when she absorbed the magical glyphs sealing the vault containing the *Book of Shadows*. Her gesture's message was unmistakable. She had earned those scars to steal that book, and now, all the power contained within its pages belonged to her.

"Angelica," I called out, "why are you doing this?"

She leaned against the stone battlement and looked down at me, her tattooed arm resting on the parapet. Around her, the archers waited like statues, their stern gazes trained on me. But Angelica's green eyes were not stern. They were alive, studying me, pulling me apart.

"Oh, Maugis," she said almost sweetly. "You look just as I remember you."

Her voice struck me like a blow. For a moment, I forgot the archers and the book and the looming siege.

"You risked much to come so close to the walls," she added. "Many of the prince's archers are itching for a fight. I don't know how long they'll listen to me before one of them decides to draw his bowstring."

I grimaced. Was that a threat? Or just a warning from someone who still harbored feelings for me?

"Why are you doing this?" I asked again.

She gave a little sigh, and I could see her hand touching the book satchel between the battlement's crenelations. "I didn't want it to be this way," she said. "Truly. But you left me no choice. None of you did. You, and Orionde, and your precious King Charles." Sudden anger flared in her gaze. "You still carry out Orionde's schemes as if she were some saint to be revered when you know the monster she has become. What she did to me, to my mother—that *cannot* be forgiven. Maugis, you chose your path. And I've chosen mine."

I clenched my jaw. "Did your mother put you up to this?"

She looked away, as if she did not want to answer.

"Where is Morgain?"

Angelica shot me a cold glare before her gaze softened a bit. "We've parted ways. She does not see the world as clearly as I do now."

I exhaled a slow breath, not having expected her last words. Morgain's influence on Angelica had been poisonous. Perhaps I could still reach her.

"So what now?" I asked. "You've cast your lot with Adalgis, like some mercenary for hire? That's not like you, Angelica, and this is not your conflict. Walk away now and let this siege come to its natural end. When it's over, I can help you. You don't have to be alone."

Her eyes brightened, and she let out a faint laugh. "Who said I was alone? *He* believes in me. He sees everything I can become."

I felt my chest tighten. "Who is he?"

Her lips curved into a ghost of a smile. "Someone who understands me. Someone who'll make me whole."

"Angelica—"

"Enough!" she snapped. "It's time to leave, Maugis,

before I walk away, and a score of them loose their arrows."

I winced. Angelica may as well have drawn her own bow and put an arrow in my chest.

"Tell your king to bring his paladins and try to take these walls. Then you'll see what happens."

This is hopeless, I thought, as Bayard had already begun turning toward the camp. I knew I could not stop him. He was a Fae horse. He had heard what she said, and he understood her threat. The next thing I knew, he sprung to a full gallop, racing toward our camp.

I was gripping Bayard's reins so tightly that my fingers pulsed with pain. All my thoughts were bent on the question whirling through my head. Who was she talking about, this man she was with? Surly not Adalgis, for he was in love with Carloman's widow. Yet if not him, then who?

The sound of hoofbeats brought my attention back to the present. I pulled on Bayard's reins to slow him down to a trot. Bradamante rode up beside me on her chestnut charger, her eyes as fiery as her auburn hair.

"Have you lost your bloody mind?" she exclaimed. "That wall is filled with archers. You could have died out there, and for what? For her?

"I wasn't—"

"No, you weren't thinking! You never do when she's involved. She's not worth your life, Maugis. She never was."

"I needed to understand why she's doing this," I stammered.

Bradamante's eyes narrowed like a hawk spotting prey. "She left you and betrayed her king! What more is there to understand? She's the enemy now, Maugis, and you are going to have to start treating her like one."

With that, she turned away and wheeled her mount.

The charger's hooves kicked up a burst of mud as it charged back toward the camp.

Sitting astride Bayard, I knew she was right. I thought of the oath I had sworn to Charles. And at that moment, having looked upon Angelica's face, I was not sure I could keep it.

CHAPTER II

THE OPENING SALVO

I bolted awake to a sound ripped from my darkest nightmares.

It began as a cacophony of high-pitched shrieks, as if the night had come alive. Shrieks mixed with thousands of squeals, raising the hair on my arms and sending a shiver down my spine. An instant later, the frightened cries of men joined this chorus of shrieks and squeals, followed by an unnerving chittering and the rat-tat-tat of scores of creatures clawing at our tent.

"What the hell?" Renaud cried out on the pallet beside me, right before the tent flap burst open under the weight of the swarm, and a horde of creatures flooded our abode, their fur bristling in the faint moonlight.

"Arrrgh!" Guichard screamed as the creatures surged over us, chittering, clawing, and biting.

One of them bit my arm, tearing through my linen tunic and sinking its teeth and claws into my flesh. The creatures were no larger than my hand, black-haired with hairless tails. Rats, scores of them, and as ravenous as vultures descending on a corpse.

I ripped one off my arm and kicked another off my leg, while my left hand shielded my eyes. The rabid beasts were clawing at my face. *They're reaching for my eyes!*

The flash of Renaud's dirk caught the edge of my vision, and I heard a rat squeal in pain. Guichard thrashed wildly, ripping rats from his chest and shoulders, his cries joining the chorus of terror that filled the camp.

I climbed to my feet, tearing a rat from my face and flinging more from my chest and limbs, but they were everywhere, scurrying up the tent walls, onto the roof, and across the floor. Renaud fought them with his dirk, slashing like a madman. A warm splash of blood streaked across my cheek as I struggled to master my fear, long enough to focus my will on the crystal set into the ring on my right hand.

Ignoring the pain from the bites and scrapes on my arms and legs, I whispered a word. *"Eoh."*

Soul light burst from the crystal, casting a wide halo across the tent. Bathed in its glow, the rats stopped squealing.

Gripping his bloodied dirk, Renaud glanced at me, stunned. Guichard appeared equally shocked as the rats slid from his limbs, their fury extinguished. One by one, they turned their gazes toward the light, mesmerized by its white glow.

My heart, still pounding from the attack, began to slow as I realized the soul light had shattered whatever sorcery had driven the rats to madness. The swarm no longer clawed or bit; they merely stared, transfixed. I recalled what Orionde had taught me: animals know the light. They recognize its source, and they will often yield to the one who wields it.

"Bloody hell, Maugis," Guichard stammered. "What in God's name is going on?"

"Sorcery," I replied. I had no doubt that was true.

"Angelica?" Renaud asked.

I swallowed hard. "Yes."

"That bitch!" Guichard exclaimed. "Or witch—that bloody bitch of a witch!"

Renaud glanced at the dozens of rats, now sitting on the floor of our tent, staring obediently into the light.

"You solved the problem here," he said, "but what about the rest of the camp?"

Outside, the cries of men and the squeals of rats filled the air like a pounding rain. I caught the acrid scent of smoke in the breeze fluttering through the tent's opening.

"Holy shait," Guichard muttered, his face gone pale. "The king!"

Guichard's words brought a new sense of urgency to our situation. I turned to the rats and yelled. *"Go!"*

As if they understood, the whole lot squealed and scattered, pouring out of the tent.

Renaud and Guichard reached for their swords. I grabbed my blackened staff and followed them, straight into chaos.

Rats swarmed across the ground, onto the tents, and around scores of men, who stabbed at them with spears and hacked wildly with swords. None of the men wore armor, having been jolted from sleep, and a few were succumbing to the sheer volume of vermin, all clawing, scratching, and biting like a murderous horde. The cries and shrieks of men and rats filled the air, mingling with thickening smoke. Several tents had caught fire, likely from braziers the rats had overturned in their frenzy. Then, to my horror, I realized that one of those tents was Charles's.

Flames were crawling up the crimson tent cloth and spewing smoke. From inside came a woman's screams, and a man bellowing curses.

Charles!

As we rounded the corner, racing toward the opening to the king's tent, I saw Roland. Gripping Durendal in his right hand, he charged inside. Renaud and Guichard burst in next. I followed them, staying focused on my soul light, for I knew I would need it now.

Through the smoke, I saw Charles at the back of the tent, roaring as he cut down rats with his sword, Joyeuse, though a half dozen clung to his tunic and gnawed at his bare legs. Behind him, a naked young woman screamed, swatting at the creatures scaling the tent's wall. Roland and Renaud were cutting a swath through the frenzied creatures, trying to get to the king. While Guichard, who had gone another way to reach Charles, was tearing at rats that must have dropped from the ceiling onto his head and shoulders.

I had but seconds to act as I willed my soul light into a sudden burst that lit up the tent. The fury drained from every rat caught in its luminous halo, and in a heartbeat, scores of the creatures fell to the floor or sat docilely, staring at its pearlescent glow.

"Be gone!" I shouted, and the rats scurried from the tent at my command.

Charles stared in stunned amazement. The woman's screams had stopped; her mouth hung open in silent wonder.

"Maugis," Renaud called urgently, "the fire!"

"Right."

I'd been so focused on the rats, I'd forgotten the flames licking up the tent's western wall and blazing around a toppled brazier on the carpeted floor.

I let my soul light fade and thrust out my staff, uttering more words of power. The air sizzled as the flames responded, drawn to my staff like water to a drain, until they curled around the staff's tip, forming a massive, blazing torch.

The heat was blistering, but I held the flames as long as I could.

I rushed out of the tent's opening, my strength nearly gone, and spotted another swarm of rats surging across the grass toward the tent behind us.

I released my will, and the fire burst from the staff like a blazing lance, engulfing the rats in a wave of flame as their death-squeals pierced the night.

My chest heaved, and I dropped to a knee. Between the effort it took to maintain my soul light and the energy spent controlling the fire, the exhaustion hit me like a blow. As I caught my breath, Guichard crouched by my side. His cheeks were red and bloodied where the rats had clawed him.

"Are you alright, cousin?" he asked.

"A bit spent," I groaned. "Go help the others."

With a smile and a nod, Guichard charged off, sword in hand, to aid the men battling the rats.

I watched as our other companions joined him: Bradamante and Olivier, their swords flashing in the moonlight; Huon with his axe, hewing through rats; and Turpin with his flanged mace, smashing them into the ground. Roland and Renaud soon joined them, along with chevaliers, archers, blacksmiths, and men-at-arms. Even the priests and nuns had entered the fray, wielding rakes and makeshift clubs. It took an hour before they had the situation under control. The surviving rats gave up the fight, as if the sorcery that fueled their rampage had faded to mist. Meanwhile, the remains of the dead vermin were piled in dark, stinking mounds throughout the camp.

By the time it was over, the army of King Charles had been battered, clawed, bitten, and harried. The nuns caring for the wounded reported that fewer than a dozen men had died, but two score or so had been blinded when the rats took their eyes. On top of that were the thousands of men who were injured and shaken as talk of the witch and her black magic spread through the camp like a foul wind.

The men were right to be afraid.

For Angelica had sent us a message, and I feared we'd only begun to understand what it meant.

IT WAS several hours past midnight when the king summoned us all to Turpin's tent.

No one had slept after our ordeal with the rats. I'd tended my scrapes, cuts, and bites with the bitter elixir I brewed from mulled blackberry leaf, mullein, and bee pollen, then rubbed a salve of beeswax, yarrow, comfrey root, and myrrh resin into the wounds. Both would help my blood to clot, a lifelong struggle, ever since I was born sickly with an illness that led my cruel father to give me my name. The midwife who delivered me said I was *"mal gist"* —lying badly—so my father named me *Maugis*.

I headed to Turpin's tent with my cousins, Renaud and Guichard. A thick fog drifted in from the riverbank, curling around the black mounds of vermin, some nearly a yard tall. The stench was already rising, a reek of damp fur, blood, and that musky, sour stench peculiar to rats. By morning, all of it would have to be burned. If not, disease might spread through the camp like wildfire. And that was the last thing we needed.

We were the last to arrive at the archbishop's tent, lit by oil lamps hanging from the tent-posts above. The king, now fully dressed, sat grim-faced beside Turpin. To Turpin's left was Naimon, the gray-haired Duke of Bavaria, leaning back in his chair, his stern face streaked with fresh claw-marks. The others stood in a half-circle around the king and his eldest advisors: Olivier, clad all in black, his dark hair falling over the forehead of his famously handsome face, without so much as a scratch; Huon, his axe-blade still speckled with blood; Roland, now dressed in his shining mail; and Bradamante, her long auburn hair pulled back into a braid, a trio of scratches raking down her left cheek.

Charles's gaze followed me as I entered the tent and stood beside Bradamante. She gave me a wide-eyed look that seemed to ask, *"Are you alright?"* I nodded in response and felt her hand touch my shoulder.

No one spoke before the king did. The silence lingered too long, broken only by the furrow of anger gathering in Charles's brow as he collected his thoughts.

"Our enemy," he said at last, "has struck us in a manner none of us could have imagined. Though our casualties were light, that was never their aim. Their goal was fear, to shake our army to its core and shatter its resolve. They cannot match our strength on the battlefield, so they've turned to craven sorcery—this devil's work—to break our siege."

He let out a shuddering breath, then slammed a clenched fist on the armrest of his chair. "We cannot let this happen again!"

"We need a bloody counterattack," Naimon growled.

Roland lifted his chin. "Lord, let me lead the strike. If we can find a way into the city after dark or before first light, with a small force of our best men, we could take the gatehouse and open the gates. If our cavalry is mounted and ready, they could reach the city while we hold the gatehouse. You've said it yourself: once we're inside, this siege will end."

"An admirable idea," Turpin said, stroking his beard. "But how will you get inside?"

"We could use ropes to scale the wall," Olivier offered.

Guichard scoffed. "And if the archers spot you on that rope? It'll be over quick, like spearing frogs in a well."

His comment earned a snicker from his brother, but the king didn't look amused.

"What if we found a way to distract the archers?" Bradamante asked. "There will be fewer of them before sunrise."

"What if the archers could not see us at all?" I said, thinking of the fog wafting in from the riverbank.

The king raised an eyebrow. "What are you thinking, Maugis?"

I drew in a breath. "We'll need a day to prepare, but using some of the secrets Orionde taught me, I'm sure I can make it work."

For the first time that night, I saw a glimmer of hope in the king's eyes.

Then I told them my plan.

CHAPTER 12

OVER THE WALLS

Preparations for our mission took all morning. Men constructed siege ladders tall enough to reach the battlements atop Verona's walls. They also procured a barge to transport the ladders down the river and commandeered several rowboats from a local fishing village. These would carry me and five of my fellow paladins, along with the men-at-arms tasked with moving the ladders into position.

After that, we waited and rested. I was apprehensive about another attack that evening. None came, but the damage from the rat swarm was worsening. Men began to fall ill. Most suffered fevers and excruciating pain in their joints and muscles, along with a fatigue so deep they could barely stand. Some broke out in burning red rashes at the sites of their bites; others vomited uncontrollably, unable to keep down even a crust of bread. Hundreds were afflicted, including Duke Naimon and Huon of Bordeaux. By sundown, the plague had touched a quarter of our entire force, and seven were already dead.

Whatever Angelica had unleashed upon us, it was more

than sorcery or vermin. It was a curse meant to rot our army from within.

And with each new victim, our mission became all the more urgent.

~

As I HAD HOPED, the fog off the river was already thick in the hours before dawn.

I traveled in the lead rowboat with my cousins, Renaud and Guichard, both of whom manned the oars. The faint splash of their blades in the water was the only sound marking our approach, much of which was swallowed by the haunting chorus of frogs croaking along the riverbanks. In the boat behind us, Roland and Olivier rowed alongside Bradamante, and behind them came two boats of men-at-arms, one towing the barge that carried the two siege ladders.

In addition to my mail hauberk, I came fully armed. I wore my ring with its stone-like crystal, gripped my blackened staff, and bore my leaf-shaped sword scabbarded at my side. In my other hand, I held a small pewter chalice, like those used for sipping spiced mead. Tonight, however, it would serve a far greater purpose, one hinted at in the apothegm Orionde had taught me long ago:

> *Stone cuts earth, staff kindles fire.*
> *Sword parts air, cup binds water.*
> *Spirit incites the power.*

The cold fog wafted around us as we drifted downriver, but above the misty curtain, I could see Verona's towering walls. I waited until we were a hundred yards away before dipping my chalice into the water. Raising it into the fog, I began swirling its contents while reciting the words of power. A subtle thrum stirred in the air before the water hissed into vapor, mingling with the surrounding fog and infusing it with the power I had summoned. The mist expanded in billowing puffs, rising into a vast cloud that towered higher with every breath, until it surged over the city walls like a great wave.

"Good God, Maugis," Guichard whispered. "All this from that tiny chalice?"

"Along with a bit of focus on my part," I muttered, already feeling the first hints of fatigue that came with using the power.

"We should have plenty of cover," Renaud said, clapping me on the shoulder. "Well done, cousin."

I nodded my thanks, then unwrapped a shard of hard, salty cheese from my belt pouch and bit into it. I would need strength for what lay ahead, and the power never came without a price.

We guided our boats through the dense fog until we found a landing spot on the riverbank, just twenty yards from the wall. Moving as quietly as we could, we disembarked while the men-at-arms lifted the siege ladders from the barge and carried them toward the base of the wall. I followed Renaud, who was little more than a shadow in the thickening mist, and felt a surge of confidence in my plan. If there were archers atop those walls, they wouldn't see us until it was far too late.

As the men-at-arms raised the siege ladders against the wall, their tops vanished into the fog.

"Brilliant plan, Maugis," Bradamante whispered in my ear as she stood behind Roland in line to scale the ladder.

I nodded my thanks, catching the warm smile on her lips. She never ceased to amaze me. Bradamante had no fear, even though she was about to climb a siege ladder and face who knows how many armed men waiting on those battlements.

Meanwhile, my stomach was twisting into a knot at the thought of what awaited us atop those walls.

We shared the ladders as we had shared the boats. Roland, Bradamante, and Olivier would climb one, while Renaud, Guichard, and I would take the other. My companions all had round shields strapped to their backs for the ascent. I wore my sable cloak instead of a shield, and had slipped my staff beneath it, fastening it securely with a leather strap across my back.

Roland and Renaud were the strongest among us, so they began the climb. Their mail hauberks chinked with each movement, and the ladders groaned faintly beneath their weight.

When Renaud had all but vanished into the fog, I started up the ladder. Hauling myself up the rungs was harder than I expected. My limbs were already heavy from the effort of summoning the mist, but I willed myself to climb.

As I neared the top, I heard the hiss of steel, followed by a man's muffled grunt. My heart beat faster. I reached the battlement and pulled myself over the crenelated parapet. Renaud emerged from the fog, blood staining his sword. A large, dark shadow lay at his feet. He held up three fingers, then made a stabbing gesture.

I pointed toward the body behind him, and he gave a nod.

A moment later, Olivier crested the parapet and dropped gracefully onto the stone walkway. Guichard followed behind me, far less graceful in his descent. Roland and Bradamante stepped out of the fog to join us, both with blood-slick blades.

Beyond the parapet, I heard the scrape of wood against stone, which meant the men-at-arms were lowering the ladders. Their task was to stash them near the base of the wall, return the boats, and take them and the barge upriver, back toward the camp. From this point, we were on our own. The only way out of Verona would be through the city gate. But to reach it, we'd have to pass four watchtowers, and none of us knew how many men might be waiting in each.

We moved in a single file. Roland led the way, followed by Renaud and Olivier. Bradamante went next. I unfastened my staff and crept behind her. At the rear, Guichard carried the king's blue pennant, its fleur-de-lis barely visible in the fog. If we reached the gatehouse, he would raise it high to signal to Charles that the gates were open and the cavalry should charge.

The fog was cold and damp as we made our way along the walkway. When we reached the first watchtower, Roland held up a hand, then slowly pushed the door open and slipped inside. Renaud and Olivier followed fast on his heels.

My chest tightened as I braced for the clang of a warning bell or a cry of alarm. But none came.

By the time I entered, three guardsmen lay dead on the floor, sword wounds in their necks and chests. The sight left a sour taste in my mouth. It felt more like slaughter than a fair fight.

But then again, this was war. And war was a bloody business.

We reached the second watchtower, only to find it strangely empty.

"Maybe they're out on the walls," Renaud whispered.

Roland nodded, cracked open the far door, and peered out.

"Two sentries," he murmured. "Though one just vanished into the fog."

"Allow me," Olivier said.

He sheathed his sword and drew a long dagger from his belt. Then he crept into the fog, as silent as a cat, with the poise of an assassin. The sentry never saw him coming. Olivier clamped a hand over the man's mouth and opened his throat with a single stroke. Then, shuffling backward, he dragged the body into the tower.

Roland eased the door shut until it was barely cracked open. A moment later, we heard a voice approaching on the walkway.

"Gundwin, where are you? I brought a torch to try to burn off this fog. Stuff's as thick as oil."

"He's heading our way," Roland whispered, stepping back from the door.

We took positions on either side of the entrance, pressed against the wall. A breath before it opened, I caught the scent of smoke. Then the door creaked, and a young sentry stepped inside, a sputtering torch in his right hand.

Guichard slammed the pommel of his sword into the back of the sentry's head, just below his helmet. The Lombard collapsed face-first onto the stone floor with an audible thud, his torch skittering across the chamber.

Olivier snatched it up and ground the flame out in the corner. Meanwhile, Bradamante was already fashioning the man's belt into a gag.

"Is he the one you saw before?" Renaud asked.

"I think so," Roland said.

I felt relieved that we had spared this one; he looked barely a day over eighteen. Though his comrade, lying dead in the corner of the chamber, did not look much older. For a moment, I wondered if Adalgis had posted his greenest soldiers on the city walls.

Bradamante had the unconscious sentry bound and gagged, though if any more sentries came across them, they'd undoubtedly sound an alarm. But it would not be the iron bell that hung in these watchchambers, for Olivier had already cut that one down and stashed it next to the extinguished torch.

We approached the third watchtower through the wafting fog, blades drawn. But when Roland pushed the door open, the chamber inside was still.

No sentries, just the firelight flickering from a brazier on an iron stand. The same one, I guessed, that the boyish sentry had used to light his torch.

Roland stepped inside first. "Empty," he whispered.

Bradamante checked the corner behind the door. "Not even a cot."

Something about the silence set my teeth on edge. We'd encountered five men through two towers, narrowly avoided detection once, and now this one stood wide open.

No resistance. No warning bell. Nothing.

A sense of unease settled deep in my gut.

As we left the watchtower and stepped onto the walkway, I caught the first glimmer of daylight to the east, piercing through the fog.

Dawn was coming.

We crept sixty yards along the battlement, only to find the door to the fourth watchchamber cracked open.

With Durendal in his right hand, Roland pressed his left palm to the door and pushed.

A startled cry rang out from inside.

My muscles tensed as Roland lunged through the doorway.

We rushed in after him. A sentry had bolted through

the far door and was sprinting down the walkway toward the hulking gatehouse. Roland stormed after him.

Olivier dashed past us, trying to catch up, with Bradamante close on his heels.

My cousins and I followed through the thinning fog.

Ahead, the sentry reached the gatehouse first and ducked through an open doorway. Roland charged in after him.

The door slammed shut, followed by the harsh scrape of iron as a bolt slid into place.

Olivier skidded to a halt; Bradamante nearly crashed into him.

From inside, Roland cried out.

I heard shouts overhead as men clamored atop the gatehouse battlement, and my heart sank.

We had walked straight into a trap.

CHAPTER 13

THE HISS IN THE WIND

I had mere seconds to act.

The tops of half a dozen bowstaves rose over the battlement. The archers were already drawing back their iron-tipped arrows, taut bowstrings creaking.

Fortunately, my leaf-shaped sword was already in my hand. I began to spin it, uttering words of power. The air sizzled as wind gathered around the blade, and before the archers could loose a single shot, I unleashed a windblast with the force of a gale.

A cry rang out from the battlement as the wind ripped helmets from heads and tore arrows from bowstrings.

Then, behind me, Renaud cried out and stumbled forward. An arrow shaft jutted from the shield slung across his back. Guichard shouted next: one shaft buried in his shield, another punching clean through his shoulder. A fourth arrow clattered against the parapet inches from Bradamante.

I spun around. Four archers stood atop the nearest watchtower, already reaching for more arrows. I spoke more words of power and summoned more wind. It howled, scattering the last of the fog before slamming into the tower and knocking the archers off their feet.

"Run!" I cried, certain the archers atop the gatehouse would be in position any second now.

"What about Roland?" Olivier shouted.

"They have him," I snapped. "Now go!"

Olivier hesitated. Renaud threw an arm around his brother and pushed him toward the watchtower. Bradamante grabbed Olivier's arm and pulled him after them.

I swept my sword in a wide arc and sent another whistling blast across the battlement above the gatehouse. It wouldn't injure the archers, but it might buy us a few more seconds.

Renaud and Guichard reached the watchtower first. As soon as they ducked through the doorway, shouts rang out, followed by the clang of steel.

The archers atop the tower must have descended into the chamber.

Olivier sprang forward, leaping through the doorway with his blade. Bradamante followed close behind, sword in hand. I rushed in after them.

Inside, one archer already lay dead. Renaud clashed with another, their swords ringing against each other. Olivier and Bradamante fought their own opponents, each archer having traded his bow for a short sword. Olivier's foe cried out as the paladin's blade punched through his throat.

But the man facing Bradamante, nearly twice her size, was holding his own. He hammered down blows, forcing her to block each one. I ended the fight by driving my blade through the links of his chainmail and into his ribs. He let out a choked scream just as Bradamante rammed her sword through his gaping mouth.

A heartbeat later, Renaud's opponent collapsed. His jaw hung unnaturally from the strike that had opened half his face.

Then came the sound of boots and shouting, echoing up from the stairwell that led to the ground floor.

"They're sending up reinforcements!" Bradamante shouted.

"To the next watchtower!" I called, remembering it had stood empty.

Guichard, red-faced and grimacing, gripped the arrow still lodged in his shoulder. Blood seeped from the wound. Renaud threw an arm around him and helped him out of the tower. Together, they ran down the walkway toward the vacant watchtower. I followed, while Bradamante and Olivier stayed behind to cover our retreat.

By the time we reached the next watchtower, men-at-arms were already storming out of the one we'd just left and onto the walkway. There had to be at least eight of them.

I darted through the open door into the chamber, where the brazier still stood on its iron stand, right where we'd left it. I thrust my blackened staff into the coals and spoke the words to gather fire. Flames burst to life and curled around the tip of the staff.

"Get behind me!" I shouted.

They obeyed, and I stepped into the doorway. The men-at-arms were barreling toward us, already halfway across the walkway. I raised my flaming staff and uttered another verse. The words sent a pulse through my veins, down my arm, and into the shaft.

With a roar, fire blasted from the staff, a jet of flame that struck the soldiers head-on.

Screams tore from their throats as the fire washed over them. One, engulfed in flame, toppled over the parapet.

Others collapsed in place, their bodies blackening as they burned.

From inside the tower, Olivier called out, "The stairwell's clear!"

"Then go," I said. "I'll follow."

The surviving soldiers, scorched but not dead, had already begun to retreat into the far tower.

I hurried down the stairwell to the ground floor. My friends were waiting. Guichard's face creased with pain.

An icy fatigue was seeping into my limbs, but I knew I'd have to draw on more of the power to help my cousin.

Olivier led the way out of the tower and into the narrow, cobblestone streets of Verona.

"We need to find an alleyway," I said. "Somewhere quiet, where I can tend to Guichard."

"That would be good," Guichard grunted, leaning on his brother's shoulder with his good arm.

"I'll find one," Bradamante said, hurrying down the street.

Dawn was still rising, so the streets remained empty, save for a stray cat watching us with curious eyes.

Moments later, Bradamante returned. "Follow me."

She led us around a corner and into a narrow alley between a church and another building, thick with shadows.

"This will have to do," I said. "Sit him down."

Renaud helped Guichard remove the shield strapped to his back, an arrow still stuck in its willow boards. Then he helped his brother to the ground, where he leaned against the brick wall of the church. Olivier took watch at the alley's entrance, while Bradamante and Renaud gathered around me and my cousin.

I sheathed my sword, set down my staff, and drew a deep breath as I dropped to one knee.

I could feel it. This might be the last of the power I could summon without collapsing. But Guichard's wound was still bleeding, a crimson stain running down his once-polished mail.

"First, we have to pull out the shaft," I said. "This will probably hurt."

Guichard nodded, sweat beading on his forehead.

"If I scream, pretend it's a war cry," he said.

"Try not to," I replied with a smile. "We're trying to hide, remember." I gripped the arrow just behind its iron head. I drew in a breath and gave it a sharp tug.

Guichard clamped a hand over his mouth to stifle his scream.

Blood gushed from the wound.

"We need to get his armor off."

Renaud helped lift the mail coat over Guichard's head while Bradamante worked at peeling away his blood-soaked gambeson and tunic.

Blood covered his bare chest, pulsing from the hole where the arrow had been.

"Hurry, cousin," Renaud urged, fear creeping into his voice.

I brought my ring to my lips and focused my will on the crystal.

"*Eoh.*"

Light burst from the stone, forming a halo around my hand. I placed my palm over the wound and let my soul light flood into the gash.

Guichard let out a long, shuddering sigh.

I began kneading the wound with my fingers, reciting a verse of power in a low, melodic chant. The bleeding stopped. As I worked the flesh, letting the power flow through me, the torn skin began to mend. Within minutes, the wound was no more than an angry red scar.

I drew in a deep breath as exhaustion seeped through my limbs.

Meanwhile, Renaud stared wide-eyed at his brother's now-healed wound. "Good God, Maugis, you did it."

"Guichard," Bradamante asked, "how do you feel?"

Guichard touched the scar, then rotated his arm. "A little stiff," he admitted. "But a lot better than it felt with that bloody arrow in it."

"You got lucky," I told him. "If it had gone in lower and punctured your lung, I'm not sure I could've fixed it. I'm afraid all I ever learned to heal was flesh and muscle. Nothing deeper than that."

"Let's get you up, brother," Renaud said, gripping Guichard's arm and helping him to his feet.

I, too, moved to stand, but as soon as I did, I staggered backward against the wall. The air around me grew thick and pungent, charged like the moment before a lightning strike. Then came a sound like a viper's hiss, and a sudden pressure hit me like a blow, shuddering through my bones.

I gritted my teeth and squeezed my eyes shut until the sensation passed.

"What's wrong?" Bradamante asked, alarmed.

When I opened my eyes, I was staring into hers. "You didn't feel that? Or hear it?"

She shook her head. "No. What was it?"

I let out a breath. "A hiss in the wind. Something's happened ..."

My words trailed off, but my thoughts turned to Angelica.

What have you done?

"What, Maugis?" Renaud pressed. "What has happened?"

Before I could answer, the sound of pounding boots echoed off the cobblestone streets. My muscles tensed.

A moment later, Olivier appeared at the mouth of the alley, his expression urgent.

"We need to move!" he said.

CHAPTER 14

THE HUNTED

"The prince's soldiers have filled the streets," Olivier explained. "I tallied thirty before I stopped counting."

He glanced at me. "Not even your magic is going to get us out of this one."

That much was true. I didn't dare draw on the power again. I was spent, barely standing as it was. But my heart pounded in my chest, and my mind willed me to move. Being hunted by hordes of enemy soldiers can have that effect on a person.

"Let's get out of here," Renaud said, drawing his sword as he headed deeper into the alley.

Guichard gathered up his mail coat, along with his bloodied gambeson and tunic, and slung his shield over his uninjured shoulder before shuffling after his brother.

I grabbed my staff, took a step to follow, and my knee buckled.

"Let me help you," Bradamante said, slipping her arm around my back to steady me.

We moved deeper into the alley's shadows, with Olivier, sword in hand, guarding the rear.

The alley bent left, and as we rounded the corner, I saw Renaud standing in an open doorway set into the church's brick wall.

"Mercifully, it was unlocked," he said. "Now get inside."

We filed through the doorway into the cool, dark hush of a church transept. Once we were all inside, Renaud quietly shut the door behind us and slid the bolt into place.

The transept was narrow, its walls rough and unadorned save for a single fresco, faded and cracked with age. Morning light had yet to reach the narrow slit windows near the apse, leaving the space cloaked in shadows, lit only by the faint flicker of an oil lamp near the altar. The air smelled of wax and mildew, with the lingering trace of incense.

"So, now what do we do?" Guichard asked.

Renaud sheathed his sword and let out a sigh. "Hide out here, for now. It may not be safe to take to the streets again until nightfall."

"What about Roland?" Olivier asked. "None of you have even said his name since he was captured."

"We've been a bit busy running for our lives, if you hadn't noticed," Guichard said.

Olivier scowled. "So we're just going to leave him with them?"

"What else can we do?" Renaud said, holding up his palms. "He's probably halfway to the prince's dungeon by now. I'd like nothing more than a daring rescue, but do you suppose the five of us can take on a palace full of guardsmen?"

"There has to be a way," Olivier insisted, anger rising in his voice.

"Look," Bradamante said, "Roland's my cousin. I swear we will save him, but Renaud is right. We'll need reinforcements, which means we have to get back to the camp."

Olivier swore under his breath. "It was as if they knew we were coming."

"How?" Guichard asked incredulously. "The only other people who knew of this plan were Huon, Turpin, Naimon, and Charles? Do you think one of them's a bloody spy?"

"Not a chance," Renaud said.

"No," I agreed. "But they *did* know we were coming. That's why the walls were so lightly manned. And with the greenest of soldiers."

Renaud shrugged. "So how did they know?"

Bradamante huffed with anger, shaking her head, as she realized what I had already suspected.

"It was that goddamned bitch," she growled.

I clasped my hands. "I don't know how Angelica's doing it, but that's the only explanation that makes sense."

But deep inside, I knew. She had the *Book of Shadows* now, and whatever secrets it held. And I was the one who had helped her claim it.

"If she knew we were coming," Guichard said, "won't she know we're hiding in this church?"

I hadn't thought of that. But she wasn't omniscient. The *Book of Shadows* couldn't have given her that much power.

Right?

I shook my head, settling on the best answer I could give. "We're in a church. That means we're on hallowed ground. It should offer some protection against the darker arts."

"I suppose that settles it then," Renaud said. "We'll

trust that Maugis is right and stay hidden until the prince's men give up the hunt. Once we're out of the city and back at camp, we'll gather reinforcements. Then we'll free Roland."

No one protested. My older cousin wasn't perfect, but he was a true leader of men. The best we had, save for Roland himself.

While we waited, I tried to rest my aching limbs, though I worked harder to stay awake. As much as I wanted to close my eyes, I couldn't risk being asleep if the prince's men came to search the church.

After several hours, I rose stiffly and wandered through the sanctuary. I made a slow lap around the nave, pausing to admire the wooden shrines to various saints along the walls, each flanked by rows of unlit candles in clay jars.

When I returned to the transept, I stopped before the faded fresco. It showed a winged angel stomping one foot down on the head of a twisted, dragon-like serpent. The angel held a long sword raised in triumph, faint white flames flickering along the blade.

"One that you recognize?" Bradamante asked, having slid quietly up beside me.

"Saint Michael and the Dragon," I replied. "I saw one like it once at the abbey of Mont-Saint-Michel."

She gave a slight nod. I had never known her to be an admirer of artwork. She was a chevalier, fond of horses, and skilled in the arts of swordcraft and battle. But as she stood beside me, even with her tangled auburn hair and her cheeks speckled with grime, I was struck by her beauty. I don't know why I hadn't noticed it more after all these years.

My gaze lingered on her until I heard the creak of a door opening somewhere in the chancel.

I spun toward the sound and reached for my blade.

Bradamante ripped hers from its scabbard. In a breath, Olivier and my cousins were at our sides, swords drawn, ready to greet our intruders.

CHAPTER 15
THE PATH THROUGH THE DEAD

A figure stepped from the shadows of the chancel and gasped, his narrow face pale as he raised his arms. His mouth, framed by a thin mustache and beard, fell open in surprise. He was a priest, slight of build, and no older than me.

Renaud lowered his sword. "Father," he said in Latin, holding up his free hand, "we mean you no harm, but we must seek sanctuary in your church."

The priest's eyes widened. "You are the Franks, the one the prince's men are searching for."

"Good observation," Olivier said, not lowering his sword an inch, as he slowly stepped toward the priest. "Now, let's not do anything foolish."

The priest glanced back at the door from which he had entered, and Olivier took another step forward.

I doubted Olivier would kill a priest in his own church, but I did not want to test that theory. I let down my sword until its tip pointed to the floor, and spoke to him. "Father, we are fleeing arrest. Under canon law, you cannot deny us sanctuary."

He paused for a moment, and I prayed the man had studied canon law.

The priest finally answered with a deliberate nod. "I will grant you sanctuary, though it would help if you put away your weapons. They should not be here in a house of God."

I gestured to Olivier, and he reluctantly sheathed his blade. The rest of us followed suit.

"Thank you," the priest said, lowering his hands. "My name is Father Laurent, and I am the presbyter of the Church of San Michele in Angusto."

So, the church was dedicated to Saint Michael. That explained the fresco.

"I am also not going to report your whereabouts to the prince's men," the priest added.

Renaud cocked his head. "You're not? Bishop Anno is in league with the prince. I figured the rest of you priests would fall in line."

Father Laurent pursed his lips. "Bishop Anno is beholden to King Desiderius, and our King, at present, is at odds with His Holiness, the Pope. I," he said, touching a hand to his chest, "remain loyal to the Holy See, and I trust in the wisdom of Pope Hadrian more than any greedy bishop. I understand that it was the Holy Father in Rome who set your King Charles on this expedition to Lombardy. So, if you are here on the Pope's business, who am I to interfere?"

Bradamante gave me a hopeful glance. Of all the priests in Verona, we had found one loyal to the Pope, not the prince's bishop.

"And besides," the priest continued, "someone needs to put an end to whatever madness has seized the prince. All this talk of a witch, and then two nights ago, the streets were thick with rats. Hordes upon hordes of them, scurrying over the city walls and shrieking into the night as if a nightmare had come to life. It was horrifying. Everyone I spoke with believes it was the work of the witch—Prince Adalgis's witch! Yet from Bishop Anno, not a word of condemnation."

"Father," Bradamante said, resting a hand on the pommel of her sword, "I swear, the next time I see that witch, it will be her last spell."

The priest raised an eyebrow while I let out a quiet sigh, for I had no doubt that Bradamante meant what she said.

"Well, Father," Guichard said with a grin and a clap of his hands, "it appears our interests are perfectly aligned."

"Uh … it seems so," Father Laurent replied.

"Great," my cousin said, rubbing his hands together. "Now, tell me, any chance you know a safe way out of Verona?"

"Hmm." Father Laurent steepled his fingers. "That depends on how comfortable you are with the dead."

OUR TORCHLIGHT WASHED over piles upon piles of human skulls. They were stacked four feet high: the skulls of men, the skulls of women, and the tiny skulls of children, hundreds upon hundreds, staring at us with empty eye sockets. Amidst the mounds of skulls were collections of other bones, piled into pits. Some held straight bones from arms and legs, while others were just jumbles of rib cages. Then, there were the hands and feet, like stacks of spider-like claws grasping at the darkness. A stench of mold and ancient decay clung to the humid air and the chamber's walls of earth and brick.

"In 565," Father Laurent explained, leading the way

with his torch through the narrow pathways that separated the mounds of human remains, "the Plague of Justinian arrived at Verona. Thousands upon thousands succumbed to the disease. There were so many dead that it was impractical to build caskets and bury them in the earth or in proper tombs. Instead, the dead were piled into plague pits throughout the city."

A shiver passed through me as my boot struck a stray leg bone, brittle as rotted wood.

The priest gestured at the chamber's ceiling. "This church happened to be built over one of those pits."

"And where exactly is this supposed to take us?" Guichard asked, holding a hand over his mouth and nose.

Father Laurent glanced back at him. "Do you feel the dampness in the air?"

We all felt it, which explained the patches of black mold speckling the walls.

"It turns out that when they dug this plague pit," the priest continued, "they breached the walls of an old Roman drainage tunnel. We are reminded of this fact several times a year, as this chamber floods every time the river overflows its banks. The tunnel drains out into the Adige. It's narrow, and you will have to crawl at times, but I suspect you can get there. I am told there is an old iron grate where the tunnel meets the riverbank. Getting past that, I cannot help you. But you somehow snuck over the guarded city walls, so I assume you are resourceful."

We followed Father Laurent deep into the plague pit, past endless mounds of bones, until we reached a spot where the brick wall had collapsed, revealing a man-sized crack that led further into the darkness.

"Beyond here is the drainage tunnel," the priest said. "I pray that you'll find yourselves safely out of the city."

"We've much to thank you for," I told him. "There

may come a time when we'll need to follow this path again. Will we be welcome?"

Father Laurent gave me a thoughtful look. "If you come in service of the Pope's cause, you will be."

I put my hands together as if in prayer. "We shall."

"Then I wish you godspeed," the priest replied. "May peace soon return to Verona."

The old drainage tunnel proved more onerous than I'd hoped. It stank of mold and refuse, with a stream of dark water running down its center. We moved in single file, crouched low, and my back began to ache within minutes. The foul air made every breath a misery. But worst of all were the low places, where we had to crawl through rancid muck that soaked our breeches and boots.

Eventually, we reached the iron grate and could see sunlight spilling through its rusted bars. The scent of the river was thick, and up against the grate, you could see the waters of the Adige. Expecting trouble at the grate, I led the way. I gave it a good jerk, but it didn't budge, which was no surprise, given that it had stood for centuries. I wasn't the strongest among us, but I didn't need to be. I was confident I could manipulate the earth around it with the power. The real obstacle was daylight. If the men on the walls saw us crawling one by one onto the riverbank in broad daylight, it would be like taking target practice. So, we waited until night fell and the fog rose from the river to make our escape.

When the time came, I summoned my soul light into the crystal in my ring and uttered the words to transform the hard earth into mud. The power worked as I'd hoped, and within moments, the grate came free.

Once we were all out of the tunnel, I wedged the gate back into place. I didn't reseal it, for as revolting as it was, we might need this path again to sneak back into the city.

Together, we crept along the riverbank under the cover of the low-hanging fog. Once we were well out of bowshot, we climbed to our feet and headed for the camp where watchfires burned into the night. As we approached the camp, my companions unslung their shields so the first watch party we encountered would know we were the King's men. Nearly every man in our army would recognize Renaud and Guichard's golden lion of Dordogne, Olivier's golden sun on a blue field, and Bradamante's silver falcon. In a short time, the plan worked when we were spotted by a half-dozen of the night's watch mounted on chargers. The lead rider raised a lantern, and its light spilled across our shields, enough to draw a cry: "Lords, you've returned!"

The riders did not mention that there were only five of us, but they had their orders ready when they found us. "Archbishop Turpin commands that we bring you to him at once!"

One of the riders galloped ahead to alert Turpin. We found him waiting outside his tent, his face lit by the blaze of a nearby watchfire.

"By God and good Saint Denis, I thought you were lost!" But Turpin's elation at the sight of us quickly faded as he wrinkled his nose. "Merciful saints, you smell as though you've climbed from a latrine trench."

"It was the only way out," Guichard replied.

Turpin winced, then his expression changed. "Where's Roland?"

"Captured," Olivier said bitterly.

The archbishop muttered a curse under his breath. "If the King's Champion has been taken, the King must know at once. And you'd best brace yourselves, he won't take the news kindly."

CHAPTER 16

ROLAND

The wine goblet spun across the tent, spraying its ruby red contents onto the carpets and walls. It hit the tapestry covering the damaged part of the canvas with a loud thud. Meanwhile, Charles's face turned a shade not much paler than the wine, his brows furrowing in fury as he roared with a voice that made my bones shiver.

"They have Roland—*my* Roland!"

He glared at the five of us, but his fiercest anger was directed at me.

"Your goddamned plan did nothing but hand them my finest warrior to use as a bargaining chip!"

His hands balled into fists. "So now what, they'll spare Roland's life if we leave Verona? So Gerberga can be set up as Adalgis's queen, while he lays claim to half my kingdom as he waits for those traitorous, soon-to-be stepsons of his to come of age? I would *never* let that happen. Yet must I sacrifice the life of the Lord Commander of the Breton March? All because you—*all of you*—let him be taken!"

The air stood still until Renaud dared to speak. "Your Highness, Roland was trying to save the mission. We'd been spotted by a sentry, and Roland chased after him. But it was a trap. Somehow they knew we were coming."

Charles's eyes narrowed into a murderous glare. "They knew? How the hell did they know?"

"The witch, My Lord," replied Bradamante, standing at attention with her arms behind her back.

"I fear," Turpin interjected, in a thoughtful tone, as if to bring down the temperature in the room, "that the supernatural influence at hand is something no one could have anticipated when we embarked on this siege. We have to consider the possibility of forces beyond just Angelica being at play, for this seems to go far beyond anything Maugis has ever told us about the teachings of the Fae."

The King turned to me. "Is this true?"

"I believe so," I said quietly. "Your Highness, I don't know how, but they were ready for us. They captured Roland, but they tried to kill the rest of us. We barely escaped."

"And only with Maugis' help," Guichard added. "Our corpses would be dangling from the gatehouse walls if it weren't for him."

Charles dragged a hand over his face and let out a sigh.

"Surely they will ransom Roland," Olivier said.

"Would you ransom him," Charles snapped, "if his life could end the siege and break a king?"

Renaud stepped forward. "Then let me lead a rescue mission, Your Highness. We have found a way in and out of the city. So allow me to take a force to free Roland and deprive the enemy of its leverage."

"And should we happen to find Adalgis along the way," Guichard interjected, making a slashing gesture across his throat, "we can end this siege right then and there."

Olivier lifted his chin and placed a fist over his heart. "Roland is like a brother to me. I failed to protect him on those walls, so I should be the one to lead his rescue. I would give my own life to save his."

"Your Highness," Renaud objected, "I outrank my friend here, it's only natural that I—"

"Enough!" Charles huffed. "The last time the five of you went on a mission, it ended in catastrophe. And if they know you're coming, *again*, then what? Half my paladins will be Adalgis's hostages, or worse, food for crows hanging off the city walls."

Turpin cleared his throat. "I think we all agree that any future plans will require careful consideration, not the least of which will be planning for the possibility they'll know in advance that we are coming. Yet I think it's fair to say that something must be done. Whatever plague those rats brought is spreading. And our army can't take many more blows like that."

My stomach clenched with mention of the plague, for the memory of the plague pit was still fresh in my mind.

"How worse has it gotten?" Bradamante asked.

Turpin's expression grew grim. "Thirty-six more have died as of this evening, and the symptoms are worsening in many of those already stricken. Though it's the crisis of faith I fear the most. I've heard that some of our men are embracing stories told by the girls around here about a wise woman who lives in the nearby hills, some healer they call the 'Morgan.' We can't have half our army putting their hopes in some pagan priestess instead of God and their King."

I was struck by the name "Morgan." Then I recalled what Angelica had told me from the wall, about her and her mother having parted ways.

Could this be Morgain?

I was beginning to contemplate the implications of that when I heard the blare of war horns outside the tent— three sharp blasts.

"All hands to arms," Renaud muttered.

"Protect the King!" Turpin said urgently.

"No, damn it!" Charles growled. "Bring me my armor and my horse!" Then he glanced at my companions and me, still armored from the mission, the worst of the tunnel's filth wiped away before we entered his tent.

"You five, go help them!" he demanded.

We didn't wait for a second command. Our swords were already drawn as we burst through the tent flaps.

Cries of "Riders!" and "To arms!" rang through the night from beyond a thick fog curling around the tents. A fog eerily similar to the one I summoned before our mission.

"Angelica—that bloody bitch!" Bradamante cursed.

As we rushed through the camp, the whinny of horses and the pounding of hooves mixed with the cries of men.

"Mount up!"

"They're on horseback!"

We were already heading for the stables. Through the murky fog, we found them awash in chaos. A host of chevaliers, some in armor, others in just the tunics and breeches, were climbing onto horses while scurrying grooms affixed saddles and bridles to other mounts. The battle's din had the horses rearing and shrieking. The acrid scent of smoke was now mixing with the misty vapour. Ahead, through the fog, I glimpsed a flash of fire.

"They're burning the tents!" Renaud said urgently.

My heart was pounding by the time I found Bayard, one of the few horses still calm amid the mayhem. He looked at me with his large, dark eyes, as if I'd kept him waiting. One of the grooms had already secured his bridle and saddle. I planted a foot in the stirrup and swung onto his back in one smooth motion. Then I slid my blackened staff into the lambskin-lined sheath strapped behind the saddle, angled away so it wouldn't jostle my leg. I didn't need to snap the reins. Bayard was already off, charging toward the battle.

Outside the stables, Bradamante caught up to us on her chestnut charger. I could not find my cousins or Olivier among the score of riders galloping toward the western edge of camp, where the attack had begun. The smoke thickened with the swirling fog, blurring the tents into shapeless shadows. But through the haze, I caught glimpses of fire. A half dozen tents blazed with flickering flames. The clang of steel on steel grew louder as we neared. Then we burst from the alleys between the tents into a cacophony of carnage and chaos.

The bodies of men and horses lay scattered across what had become a battlefield. Through the mist, I counted three score or more of our soldiers fighting on foot and horseback, battling twice their number. Shapes flickered in and out of view, some two dozen enemy riders darting through the fog, thrusting spears or hurling flaming brands into tents. Maybe half our men wore armor; the rest fought in tunics or nightclothes against skirmishers from Verona in full chainmail. Spears and swords flashed in the firelight, and the air stank of sweat and scorched canvas.

Bradamante ripped her sword from its scabbard and charged, swinging it into the first Veronese horseman she saw. I drew my own blade, telling Bayard, "Let's drive them back!"

Bayard answered the call by sinking his teeth into the rump of the nearest enemy horse, causing it to buck, and leaving its flailing rider unprepared when I stuck my sword into his side. The horsemen who rode with us barreled into enemy riders, and I glimpsed Bradamante's blade arc into another skirmisher, spraying blood. I had no shield, which put me at a distinct disadvantage against riders with spears, but I had Bayard. Faster, stronger, and smarter than any mortal horse, he dodged to the side of an enemy's spear thrust, then bit the man on the shoulder and tore him from his mount, before a swift stomp of Bayard's hoof ended any further threat the man posed.

From behind me rose a new battle cry. I craned my neck to see Olivier, Renaud, and Guichard leading a dozen more chevaliers into the fray. They crashed into the skirmishers like a wave of hooves and steel. Some of the enemy wheeled their mounts to flee the battle. But ahead, a furious fight unfolded through the ghostly mist. A score of Veronese riders clashed with an equal number of our men, but around them lay just as many dead, and I quickly saw why. A large warrior on a huge, black destrier was hammering swordblows into our chevaliers, cutting men down with deadly strikes. His face was hidden beneath a helm crowned with a blood-red plume. He roared with fury—*or was it delight?*—as he hewed through men with a bloodslick broadsword.

I lost sight of him as another skirmisher came at me, this time with a sword. I blocked the blow with my own, just before Bayard reared up and kicked the enemy rider in the head. By the time I found the plumed rider again, more dead men had joined the grisly circle of bodies around him and his fellow horsemen. With a brutally efficient strike, the plumed rider took another man's head clean off his shoulders. Meanwhile, Olivier and my cousins were fighting their way toward him, but the Veronese were defending their captain, as he hacked into the neck of a chevalier's horse, killing the beast and sending its rider flailing onto the turf, into a storm of pounding hooves.

I was too far away to reach the plumed rider, and had no doubt he could best me with his broadsword, but I had other weapons. I spun my blade in a narrow circle and whispered the words to summon the wind. The air sizzled around me as I felt the power pulse into my sword, whipping the air around it. With a cry, I thrust the blade forward and released the windblast aimed straight at the plumed rider. The blast was strong enough to rip the man from his saddle, and once he was down, our chevaliers would have the advantage. The windblast howled toward the plumed rider, but he turned, unnaturally calm, and raised a gauntleted hand. Eldrich blue fire sparked from his open palm. The air thrummed, and to my horror, I felt my control of the wind slip away. The blast dissipated into nothingness.

That's not possible, my mind screamed.

Another battle cry filled the air, and I glimpsed a column of reinforcements riding from camp, with Turpin and Charles at its head. The plumed rider hesitated, as if he knew now that he was outnumbered. Then he tore the red-plumed helmet from his head—and I gasped.

It was Roland.

His face was unmistakable, twisted in a grin that didn't belong to the man I knew.

With a fierce roar, he struck down another of our riders with his sword, one I recognized now, for I had held it myself.

Durendal.

Roland jerked on his stallion's reins, turning the black beast from the battle, and charged into the fog towards Verona. A dozen of his riders followed close behind, and in a breath, the remaining skirmishers disengaged and fled, though the damage was done. Scores of ours lay dead, and all of our riders had ceased their charge. My friends—Olivier, Renaud, Bradamante, and Guichard—stared in horror as they watched Roland ride off with the enemy horsemen.

Charles and Turpin sat frozen in their saddles, the shock plain on their faces.

My thoughts reeled. Just moments ago, we had spoken of rescuing him, but now Roland *was* the enemy.

And the wound he'd inflicted struck as deep as a mortal blow.

CHAPTER 17

THE MORGAN

In the aftermath of the attack, we gathered in Turpin's tent. Charles sat with his arms crossed, staring at the woven carpet beneath his boots. The only sound was the faint crackle from the braziers, their coals casting flickering shadows on the canvas walls. Olivier, Bradamante, and my cousins joined the three of us, sitting silently in a circle, their faces as downcast as the King's.

"How could this happen?" Charles finally asked. His gaze fixed on me.

I shook my head, still feeling the crushing weight of what happened in my bones. "Angelica must have done something to him. Driven him to this madness."

Bradamante clenched her jaw. "Then why don't we just kill her? Wouldn't that break the spell?"

Her words stung. I sighed. "I don't know. I don't even know what we're dealing with. Or if that was truly Roland."

Olivier frowned. "What are you saying? We all saw him. It was Roland."

I rubbed my face. "I summoned the wind against him. It should have ripped him from the saddle. But it didn't. He stopped it. He summoned power of his own and just … dispelled mine, like it was nothing."

A few of them gasped.

"That's impossible," Charles said, shaking his head.

Turpin's eyes narrowed. "Maugis, are you certain?"

"Yes. I felt it."

Renaud threw up his hands. "So now Roland's a sorcerer?"

"Bloody hell," Guichard muttered. "He was already too damn good with a sword. Now he can summon fog, start magic fires, do whatever the hell he wants?"

Olivier's voice dropped. "If his magic is stronger than yours …"

He didn't finish the thought. He didn't need to.

"We're dealing with something beyond nature," Turpin said. "Maybe it's not Roland after all."

"Don't be ridiculous!" Renaud snapped. "We *saw* him!"

But sometimes the eyes can be fooled, I thought. It had happened before, in Rosefleur, when Morgain tricked me with her glamour.

Morgain …

I recalled what I learned before the attack, about the healer they called the Morgan.

"There might be a way to find out what's happened," I said slowly. "Turpin, you told us about a wise woman in the hills, the one they call the Morgan. I think I know who she is. Back in Rosefleur, there was a Fae named Morgain. She was close to Angelica. They left Rosefleur together."

Bradamante wrinkled her brow. "If she's close to Angelica, how could you ever trust her? They're probably working together!"

"I don't think so," I said. "When I spoke to Angelica at the walls, she said something that made me believe they'd had a falling out. That might explain why Morgain is nearby. If I could find her in those hills, maybe I could find a way to save Roland."

"If she's one of the Fae," Turpin said, scratching his beard, "and if the Fae are truly what you say they are, then she might be our best hope."

Charles rested his chin on his fist, thinking it through. After a moment, he said, "Go find her. Leave at first light, but return as quickly as you can."

"Yes, my lord," I replied.

"I'm going, too," Bradamante said.

All eyes turned to her.

"That's not a good idea," I said before I could stop myself. "Morgain knows me. But she's dangerous, more dangerous than any Fae I've ever met."

Bradamante glared. "Roland is my cousin. I *am* going, damnit, and I dare any one of you to try and stop me."

According to the old woman we spoke with in the village on the way to the hills, the Morgan lived in a cave set into a limestone cliff at the foot of a forested slope above the Fumane valley. She spoke of the Morgan with great reverence. Just a week earlier, they had brought a young girl to the cave, so stricken with illness that she stood at death's door. But the Morgan cured her. The entire village saw it as a miracle. Some believed the Morgan was an angel sent from the heavens. Others thought she was a priestess of the old gods, who ruled the world before the coming of Christ. A few even claimed she was the mother goddess of the Gauls, who lived in these hills before the Romans.

If only they knew how close these beliefs were to the truth.

I rode Bayard up a shepherd's trail that wound its way into the hills, framed on both sides by twisting oaks. I wore my armor and sable cloak, with a satchel slung over my shoulder, the one that held the leather-bound book Orionde had given me when I first began my apprenticeship. Bradamante followed close behind on her chestnut charger. She came dressed for battle.

As the sun dipped toward the western horizon, we reached the cliff the old woman had described. The trees that had grown thick along the slope gave way to ridges of limestone speckled with dark green moss. Soon, the path grew too rocky for our horses to continue. Bradamante tethered her mount to a beech tree. Bayard needed no such restraint. I simply told him to stay, and he nodded thoughtfully, fixing me with those large, black eyes.

The path cut through a narrow ravine, and as we advanced, I began to sense the subtle thrum in the air that always preceded a gateway to the Otherworld. Before long, we found the cave, its mouth cloaked in shadow. As we stepped closer, I heard a faint buzzing, like a hive of bees, and glimpsed a thick veil of mist hanging just a half-yard inside the entrance.

"What is that?" Bradamante asked, her brow creased.

"A sign that I was right," I said. "The mist is a telltale mark of the Fae. It always guards the entrances to the Otherworld."

Bradamante cocked her head. "Are you being serious?"

I nodded. "It protects the gateway to Rosefleur, and it serves as a warning. Those who don't know the way through often meet a grim fate. That's why I need you to wait here."

She grabbed my wrist. "I'm going with you."

I tried to pull free, but her grip tightened.

"It's not safe for you in there," I said.

"I don't care."

One look at the fire in her eyes told me I wasn't going to win this fight.

I exhaled. "Fine."

She let go of my wrist. "I'll need to do something to get us through." I brought my ring with the crystal to my lips, cleared my mind, and whispered the word, "*Eoh.*" White light burst from the gemstone.

I turned back toward her. "You should hold onto my hand."

I wrapped my fingers around hers. Despite the calluses from years of swordplay, her touch felt unexpectedly pleasant. But that feeling was quickly replaced by the knot tightening in my stomach as we stepped into the mist.

My soul light parted the vapor like a curtain. A chill prickled across my skin as we crossed the threshold hand in hand. Then I sucked in a breath at what awaited us inside.

The chamber was as vast as a cathedral's nave. Instead of limestone, towering columns of crystal rose around us, reaching toward a domed ceiling studded with stalactites. The crystals glowed faintly, mauve and green shafts of light shimmering from their cores, while a warmer, golden radiance spilled down from the stalactites above. Along the walls, veins of blue-tinted crystal pulsed like living stone. Near the far end of the cavern, this strange array of colors danced across the surface of a still, black pool, if it was water at all. For it looked darker than any water had a right to be. Meanwhile, motes of yellow light flitted through the chamber like fireflies, blinking in and out of existence. Yet despite the glow, the air held the silence of a tomb.

"My God," Bradamante whispered. "It's beautiful."

And it was. Not windblown or desolate like the plains

near Rosefleur, nor the hellscape of the Riverlands deep within the Otherworld. This place gave meaning to the word *magical*.

I found myself still holding Bradamante's hand. Her touch was warm. But I let go the instant I heard the soft patter of bare feet on stone.

She emerged like an apparition from the shadows between two crystal columns, tall, slender, and draped in a black dress that clung to her perfect form. Her hair, long and dark as obsidian, shimmered with hints of the cave's shifting colors. But it was her face, pale and hauntingly beautiful, that struck me. It was not the proud, inscrutable face of the Fae woman I had known at Rosefleur, but one marked by a profound and quiet sorrow.

"Maugis," she said. "I trust you've come about Angelica."

CHAPTER 18

A DARKER PLAN

"I need to know what's happened to her," I told Morgain. "Why is she doing this?"

A flicker of a frown crossed Morgain's face before her gaze sharpened, fixing on Bradamante. "Who is she?" The words came out more as a demand than a question.

My muscles tensed. Bradamante shot me a wary, sidelong glance.

"Her name is Bradamante," I said. "She's a chevalier in the service of King Charles of Francia."

"Tell her to leave," Morgain said coldly.

Bradamante's hand drifted to the pommel of her sword. "I'm not going anywhere."

A faint smile curved Morgain's lips. She raised her right hand, and eldritch blue flames danced across her fingertips. With a single, fluid motion, she traced a glowing circle in the air.

Bradamante froze.

My breath caught in my throat.

Then Morgain etched a symbol inside the circle. It was

103

not a letter from any mortal alphabet, but a glyph pulsing with preternatural light.

"Leave us," she said. "This is a private affair."

Bradamante's eyelids fluttered, and a moment later, her knees gave out. I lunged to catch her as she collapsed into my arms. My heart pounded as I eased her to the ground, until I saw her chest rise and fall with steady breaths.

"No need to fear," Morgain said. "She's merely asleep. I can wake her with a snap of my fingers."

I nodded, having no choice but to take her at her word.

"Now follow me," she said, turning away. "We have much to discuss."

She sauntered past luminescent crystal columns toward the black pool at the far end of the grotto. I cast one last glance at Bradamante, still sleeping peacefully on the stone floor, then hurried to catch up.

"This grotto," Morgain said, gesturing around us, "was one of my favorite places after our banishment. I've always found it to be one of the most beautiful places in the Otherworld. But it was too small to shelter our tribe of refugees, so we eventually made a new home beneath one of the Pillars of Hercules, near the shores of Atlantis. Still, I loved this place. It's where Angelica and I came after we left Rosefleur."

She nodded toward the pool. Now that we stood near it, it looked less like a basin and more like a sunken lake. Its surface was still and impossibly dark, like it had been filled with ink.

"It's fed by the waters of the Acheron," she said. "Not the best place for a swim, I'm afraid."

She rounded one of the columns and led me toward a broad alcove. The crystal walls here gave off a soft blue glow, and steam curled gently from the ground. At its center was a smaller pool, its water silver and shimmering.

"This one," she continued, "draws from a hot spring in the mortal plane." She gave the pool a wistful glance. "It's the only thing that brings me any comfort now."

She stepped into the alcove, and I followed. More chambers branched off through archways formed by the natural curve of the crystal walls. In a smaller recess at the far end stood a rack of garments. They were robes and dresses of black, white, and gray, their muted colors stark against the brilliance of the grotto.

Then, without a word, Morgain slipped out of her black dress and let it fall to the floor. I froze, startled, as she stood naked before me, her form flawless and sculpted like the statues of goddesses from the temples of old. Heat stirred within me, low and sudden.

She lowered herself into the pool, the silver water rising until it covered her chest. Her hair fanned out across the surface, catching the blue glow of the crystals like strands of starlight.

"Join me," she said.

Resistance seemed futile. And I needed answers, no matter what it might take to get them.

I unfastened the brooch of my sable cloak and let it fall to the floor. I unbuckled my sword belt and set it on my cloak. Then came my mail hauberk, pulled over my head with a dull clatter, followed by the padded gambeson beneath. I peeled off my linen tunic and stood bare-chested before her. My boots and breeches came next.

When I was clad in nothing but my ring, I stepped into the pool. The water was hot, but soothing, and I sank slowly until it rose to my neck.

"What's happened to Angelica?" I asked, forcing down the desire burning in my veins.

Morgain glanced away, her eyes falling to the pool.

"It's all my fault," she said softly. "I led her to the book."

"The *Book of Shadows*?"

She nodded, her gaze returning to mine.

"After Orionde imprisoned me in the Riverlands, and after she murdered Accolon and took our daughter, my grief was unimaginable. The loneliness of that place was like a weight I could never lift. But I was never truly alone. The denizens of that realm are the stuff of nightmares. And yet, the one who found me seemed … different. He wore a dark cowl and the skin of something vaguely manlike, like the old legends of Charon the Ferryman brought to life."

She stepped closer to me, and I drew a deep breath.

"He was the one who reminded me of the book," she said. "The one we tried so hard to destroy after the fall of Atlantis. The book that would not burn. He said it held secrets that could free me from the Riverlands and banish the one who sent me there. And I believed him. He was … persuasive. And in the end, he spoke the truth. Or at least half of it."

"Who was *he*?"

"Astaroth. The second son of Samyaza, the one you call the Dragon. I once knew him, long ago. First as a boy, then as a man. He was so much like his father: handsome, flawless, infinitely proud. A prince among giants, born to believe he was a god, destined to rule the mortal world. In the war that led to our banishment, his mortal body was destroyed by the Archangel Raphael. But his spirit survived, and he became a demon, what some now call the Grand Duke of Hell."

Her voice dropped to a whisper.

"But the creature who found me in that wretched body in the Riverlands did not act like a demon. He seemed to care. He offered help. He told me how to reach Angelica. And you made that possible when you triggered the glyph in my cottage near Rosefleur. Astaroth knew she could use the book to free me."

She paused, her eyes searching mine.

"He allowed me to see my daughter again, and to enact my revenge on Orionde and Una. I thought I had been made almost whole. Angelica had her father's fighting spirit, but in every other way, she was mine. Bold, beautiful, ambitious. She reminded me of the person I once was, in the days when the world was still young.

"Our first two years together were glorious. I taught her more of the mysteries, secrets that Orionde would never have revealed to her. In return, she brought me stories from the world outside. Once upon a time, our kind shaped the affairs of men. I miss those days. But I enjoyed her tales of princes and kings, of popes and bishops, all the players in the grand game of crowns."

"What happened between you two?" I asked.

Morgain let out a sigh. "Angelica was always a deeply curious person. Even with the mysteries I taught her, her appetite for knowledge was not satisfied. So she turned to the *Book of Shadows*. Astaroth had learned the secrets held within its pages from his father. Let's just say there was a reason Orionde kept that book hidden for so long. I should have known better, but I did not stop her. Over time, her moods darkened, and at times, her temper flared like a midsummer storm. She spoke of the book as if it were talking to her. As if *he* were speaking to her from the pages. I threatened to take the book away, which only fueled her fire. Then one night, our argument became an inferno. I feared I was losing her, and I was right. I seized the book, and she stormed out of the grotto. But she had already memorized the secret she would use to defeat me upon her return. The one she used at Rosefleur. The violet fog that puts our kind into the Sleep. When I awoke from it, she was gone. And so was the book."

I remembered that violet fog, the day I found the Sisters of Orionde strewn like corpses across Rosefleur's floors. But it was her belief that *he* was speaking to Angelica through the pages that chilled me the most.

He believes in me, she had said, standing atop Verona's walls.

The implication settled in my bones like ice, despite the steam rising from the pool.

"I later learned," Morgain continued, "that she had joined the court of King Desiderius. I believe he even took her as one of his consorts. I imagine she went willingly, only to bend him to her will. For now, she's the one moving the pieces on the board. I even suspect she had a hand in luring your King Charles here, all the way to Verona's walls."

I shook my head. "Why would she do this?"

Morgain's gaze narrowed. "Because *he* is manipulating her through the pages of that book. And I fear this is only the beginning of a darker plan. One I never saw coming … not through the haze of my grief and despair."

"What concern would Angelica and Astaroth have with the King of Francia?"

Morgain rose from the pool, water streaming down her flawless form.

"I do not know," she said. "But you and I can find out —*tonight.*"

CHAPTER 19

INTO THE NIGHT

"It's called astral projection," Morgain explained. "The spirit leaves the body to travel through the spirit realm, which surrounds the mortal world, unseen, like the air itself."

We wore white linen robes, seated on furs atop a bed in a chamber apart from the hot spring. The linen clung to my damp skin, as it did to Morgain's, thin and opaque against her breasts. But the desire I'd felt upon seeing her naked had been replaced by a deep and growing curiosity.

"It's how," she continued, "I was able to project my spirit from the Riverlands to reach Angelica in her dreams, after you triggered the ward in my cottage. And it's how I've been watching her, now and then, since she left this grotto. I've only known a few mortals who could master the art. There isn't time to teach you. But I can take you with me."

"How?" I asked.

"Lie back. Clear your mind, as you do when summoning your soul light. Then take my hand, and don't let go. I'll do the rest."

I did as she instructed. Closing my eyes, I heard her recite words of power I had never spoken, a verse with the melody of a song. She took my hand. At first, her skin was cold, but it was quickly replaced by a strange, tingling warmth that crawled up my arm and spread through my body.

Then I felt myself rising, lighter than air.

When I opened my eyes, we were ascending toward the chamber's rough-hewn ceiling, crusted with glowing green crystal. Then, effortlessly, we turned upside down, and I found myself staring down at our bodies, lying side by side on the bed, eyes closed, still holding hands.

Then I noticed the silver cords.

No thicker than a rope, the pearlescent cords tethered whatever we were now to the bodies beneath us.

"What is this?" I stammered.

"The silver cords connect our spirits to our bodies," Morgain said. "But don't worry, they won't keep us here. They can stretch for leagues without breaking."

I stared at mine in awe, watching it arc toward my heart in the body below. "It can be severed?"

"Yes."

"What happens then?"

"Without the spirit, the body dies."

Those words should have sent a chill up my spine. But I felt nothing. Neither warm nor cold, as if my spirit form no longer registered temperature. The only sensation I had was Morgain's hand in mine, humming with the strange energy that bound our spirits together.

We began drifting from the chamber, gliding five feet above the hot spring and into the larger crystal cavern. It was as if we were gliding like birds, but without wings. Lighter than air but carried by an unseen current.

As we neared the mist-veiled entrance to the grotto, I

glimpsed Bradamante still lying on the ground, motionless in sleep. A faint white glow shimmered across her skin.

"What is that?" I asked.

"Proof that she's alive," Morgain replied. "That glow is her spirit. One of many things you can perceive from within this realm."

We drifted past her and, in a breath, passed through the mist. We emerged into the open night, floating above the hillside beneath a star-filled sky.

"Hold tight," Morgain said. "It's time to fly."

I felt a pulse of energy, and then we soared. The hill dropped away into darkness, the ground vanishing beneath us. I've ridden fast on Bayard, fast enough for the wind to burn my skin. But this was twice as fast. Maybe three times. And yet I felt nothing.

Miles ahead, a reddish glow flickered across the Lombard countryside. Fires. Beyond them, smoke blurred the sky, rising before what looked like an island of stone.

Verona.

Which meant the fires were burning before the city walls.

In the area of our camp!

My heart should have been pounding, but I had no heart in my spirit form. Still, my mind screamed, filling with dread at what was happening outside the city walls.

We sped toward the fire. Miles passed beneath us in a blur. As we swooped lower, our pace slowed. Ahead, our camp sprawled fifty yards below. The timber watchtowers were ablaze, as were rows of tents at the camp's head. Smoke mingled with swirling fog as men rushed between the tents, weapons in hand, racing toward the flames.

We soared over the animal pens, where panicked horses shrieked in fear. Many were being saddled as riders galloped toward a growing melee. The sounds of battle swelled as we plunged through the smoke, untouched by the searing heat burning through tentcloth and timber.

We emerged above a clash of horsemen, scores on each side. Bodies of men and horses were strewn across the battlefield. Among them wandered ghost-like spirits, pale and weightless, unseen by the living.

"The souls of the slain," Morgain observed, without a hint of concern.

The spirits did not join the fight. They drifted silently through the carnage, as if unsure how they'd ended up there. But around them, the battle raged on.

We hovered now above the field. A horn sounded behind us. I craned my neck to look as a fresh wave of riders thundered from the camp. Olivier led them, with Charles and Turpin at his side.

At the horn's cry, many of the attackers wheeled their mounts. And that's when I saw the rider in the plumed helm.

Roland.

The ground around him was littered with corpses, both man and horse. Blood glistened on Durendal's blade. He sheathed the sword, seized his reins, and turned his warhorse toward the city. At least three score of the Lombard horsemen followed him at full gallop.

"Catch up to that rider in the plumed helm," I said to Morgain.

"Who is he?"

"Roland," I replied. "He was one of ours. But something's turned him against us."

Morgain gave me a curious look, and then we were speeding forward.

We caught up quickly, though Morgain kept us at a distance, hovering forty feet above the ground.

Up ahead, within the archway of the hulking gatehouse, the city gates stood open just wide enough for two riders to pass through side by side. Roland charged into the breach. We soared over the gatehouse as he emerged on the far side, never slowing his mount, whose hooves thundered across the cobblestone streets.

We followed, gliding above rooftops of slate and terracotta tile. The glow of lanterns hanging from lampposts cut through the shadows blanketing the alleyways, and beneath us, I could swear I saw translucent spirits lingering in some of those shadows, half-hidden from sight.

Roland rode toward an enormous arena, three tiers of archways stacked one atop the other in a vast circle. He veered right, curving around the structure as we flew over the sand-covered arena floor where gladiators had once fought in Roman times.

From there, he spurred his horse down another street and through the open gateway of what appeared to be an older city wall. He galloped down a stretch of cobblestones before ascending a winding street that zigzagged past buildings and rows of spire-like cypresses. The road climbed steadily toward a stone fortress, the kind the Romans had left scattered across much of Europe.

We rose higher, keeping a safe distance as he reached the fortress's open gates.

Floating over the battlements, twenty feet high, we entered a lantern-lit courtyard. At the far end stood a palace-like keep, three stories tall. Beside it stretched thatch-roofed stables, large enough to house twenty horses. The stables ended at the base of a tower that rose two stories higher than the keep, its peak crowned with an elaborate timber rookery that resembled a cluster of birdhouses. High above it, a banner bearing Desiderius's golden eagle rustled in the night breeze.

Roland reined in his mount, and a troupe of grooms

rushed from the stables to meet him. We drifted closer as he dismounted with casual ease, tore off his helmet, and tossed it to one of the grooms.

Beside me, Morgain gasped.

"Lancelot," she breathed.

"Who?"

She shook her head. "It looks just like him. But it's been almost three hundred years ..."

I hadn't heard that name before. But whatever she thought she saw, I was certain of one thing: this was Roland.

He turned from the grooms and headed toward the tower. After climbing a short flight of steps, he opened a sturdy wooden door and disappeared inside.

"Can we follow him?" I asked, afraid our trail had ended.

"Of course."

As we drifted down toward the door, I could hear the ravens screeching from their cages in the rookery atop the tower, as if the birds could sense our astral forms. I prayed Roland could not hear them from inside, yet even if he did, who knows what scares birds in the night?

When we reached the door, we passed straight through it, emerging into a foyer dimly lit by rushlights. From an archway at the far end, I heard the clomp of boots on stone stairs. We glided forward and floated up the spiral staircase until Roland came into view once more.

We were so close now that I could see the glow of his spirit clinging to his skin. But unlike Bradamante's pale white aura or that of the wandering souls we'd seen on the battlefield, Roland's glowed with a vibrant violet hue.

The stairs ended at a landing, also lit by rushlights. An archway to the left led to another flight of stairs, but Roland strode into a chamber across the way.

A voice called from within: "Has my lord returned triumphant?"

The sound struck me like a blade.

Angelica.

Morgain shot me a look, one eyebrow raised.

"Victorious and hungry," Roland replied. His voice was deep, husky, sharpened by an edge I didn't recognize.

We drifted through the doorway into a sitting room lit by oil lamps and comfortably furnished. Roland unclasped his sword belt and let it fall to the floor with a thud. He grabbed a carafe of wine from a small table and drained it in one long gulp.

From a doorway that led into what must have been the bedchamber, Angelica sauntered out.

My jaw went slack.

She wore nothing but the symbols tattooed down her right arm and a look of pure seduction. "How hungry *are* you?"

Roland let the empty carafe slip from his hand. It shattered on the stone floor, the remnants of wine splattering the rushes. He stripped off his chainmail, then his gambeson and tunic, until he stood bare-chested before her. The violet light pulsed from his skin with every breath.

Angelica leapt into his embrace. They kissed—deeply, hungrily—the way she had once kissed me. Had I still been in my body, my heart might have stopped. I watched in stunned silence as she pulled down his breeches and backed him into the bedchamber.

They fell onto a four-post bed, her legs wrapping around his hips, her lips parting only to breathe and moan. They moved together in a rhythm I knew far too well, my former lover with one of my dearest friends.

I might have retched if my astral form had a stomach. But all I could do was watch in horror.

The violet glow that clung to him began to swell, taking on the form of something manlike, larger than Roland, more muscular, like another body layered over his. Angelica's pale skin glowed under it, bathed in purple light.

Then the form sharpened.

Broad shoulders. A strong neck. Ears tapering to fine points.

He turned his head, slowly, as if he could see us.

A second face, overlaid with Roland's, stared at us. Violet. Handsomely cruel. And where his eyes should have been, red irises flickered like flames.

"*Astaroth,*" Morgain gasped.

"What is it, my lord?" Angelica asked, alarmed.

"He can see us," Morgain hissed.

The demon possessing Roland snarled. Words of power began to spill from his lips.

With a sharp jerk, Morgain yanked me from the chamber. We burst through two stone walls as if they were made of air, and the next thing I knew, we were soaring over the rooftops of Verona.

Morgain was flying faster than she ever had before. In an instant, I understood why.

They erupted from the tower in a burst of flame, half a dozen of them, shooting after us like burning arrows.

My eyes widened.

Their wings were batlike, flapping frantically. Their mouths were surrounded by writhing feelers. They were as large as vampire bats, and despite Morgain's speed, they were gaining.

"What are those things?" I cried.

"Gallu demons!" she shouted back. "They feed on the silver cords!"

I tore my gaze from the oncoming demons to look at

the silver cord attached to my astral form, stretching for miles toward the grotto, a thin thread disappearing into the night.

We streaked over the city walls, past the smoldering remains of our camp. Behind us, I could hear the beating of wings as the fiery swarm closed in. Fifty yards away, gaining ten with every breath.

We raced over the dark countryside. In the starlight, I could just make out the silhouette of the hills ahead. The demons were barely twenty yards behind.

"Hurry!" I shouted to Morgain, remembering her words.

Without the spirit, the body dies.

Her grip tightened around my hand as we surged over the foothills and began to climb. Sensing the nearness of their prey, the demons surged forward.

Then they struck.

I cried out as claws latched onto my limbs, tearing into my astral flesh, if you could even call it that. Three of them crawled up my back like insects, their mouths sucking at my skin with those writhing feelers. To my horror, I realized they had no eyes. Just smooth, eyeless heads, like some foul fusion of lamprey and bat, set ablaze with magical fire.

One latched onto my silver cord.

I gasped, not from pain, but from something worse: a cold deeper than ice spreading through my torso. It was as if they were leeches, draining my life force straight from the cord.

I writhed in terror. There was nothing I could do. The cold spread through what should have been veins, climbing into my neck, my head, my eyes. My vision dimmed. Darkness closed in.

Then I screamed.

CHAPTER 20

THE DARKNESS BEFORE THE DAWN

My eyes flew open. Above me, the luminescent green ceiling of Morgain's bedchamber glowed softly in the grotto's half-light.

Something clung to my chest, tight, wet, and cold. I clutched at it instinctively. My fingers wrapped around something slick and slimy, like a wet fish. I yanked it off and felt tiny claws detach from my skin.

To my horror, I was holding one of the Gallu demons. Its wings hung limp, and the tentacles around its lamprey-like mouth dangled uselessly.

"It's dead," Morgain said, sitting up in the bed beside me. "The Gallu are creatures of the astral plane. They can't survive in the mortal world."

With a shudder, I flung the corpse away. My heart, which had been pounding, slowly began to settle.

"I thought we were done for," I muttered.

"Nearly so," she replied. "Another minute and that creature would have gnawed through your silver cord. We reached our bodies just in time. I drew us back before it could finish."

I sat up in bed and held my head in my hands. Memories of the last half hour rushed forward like a flood. Astaroth's handsomely cruel face overlaid on Roland's own. The image of him ravishing Angelica, and her relishing every minute of it. And her voice:

Has my lord returned triumphant?

"She called him lord," I said aloud.

Morgain ran her fingers down her face. "It's worse than I imagined," she whispered. "I didn't see it before, but this must have always been his plan …"

"What do you mean?"

"In the Riverlands, Astaroth preyed on my grief. He convinced me to reach out to Angelica, to guide her toward the *Book of Shadows*. He knew she could use it to free me, and at the time, that was all I wanted. To be free. To be with my daughter."

Her voice grew quiet.

"But he knew the book would sink its claws into her. That it would twist her thoughts, bend her will. She became so obsessed with it that she chose it over me. But it wasn't truly her choice. It was his. Astaroth must have been poisoning her mind all along. His goal was to come here, to cross into the mortal world. And in your friend Roland—this Lancelot reborn—she found him the perfect vessel. What he plans to do with that vessel, who knows?"

That's when it struck me.

I knew.

Orionde had made her plan clear. Charles was to forge an empire. And I was to help him do so. Somehow, Astaroth discovered this, and he meant to shatter this empire before it could ever be formed.

Yet if the demon was as powerful as Morgain claimed, how could we possibly stop him?

I must have spoken the question aloud, because Morgain answered me.

"There is a way," she said.

~

"You'll want to write this down," Morgain instructed me.

We sat in her bedchamber. I'd retrieved my satchel and the book where I recorded everything the Sisters of Orionde had ever taught me. I leafed through it for a blank sheet of vellum, then uncorked my jar of ink and drew my quill. When I was ready, I wrote the title of her lesson just as she spoke it:

On the Warding and Binding of Demons.

Morgain rose, still dressed in her thin linen robe, and began to pace.

"The only way to save your friend Roland is to drive the demon out. The priests of this age—those who call themselves exorcists—think they know how, but their methods are crude and often ineffective. Even when they do manage to cast a demon out, they have nowhere to put it. So they let it loose into the world, like someone releasing a man-eating wolf. Completely ill-advised, I assure you."

She strode to a shelf built into the chamber wall and retrieved a gray stone box no larger than a brick, etched with arcane symbols.

"To do this properly, you must trap the demon in a new vessel. Sometimes they're cast into animals. You've heard the tale of the swine, no doubt."

I recalled that one from the gospels. "The Savior cast a

legion of demons into a herd of pigs. The swine all went mad, then stampeded into the sea and drowned."

"Good," Morgain said, "but you're not the Savior, and trapping a demon within a beast has great risks. They don't always surrender and drown themselves in the sea. No, inside a beast, a demon can still cause havoc. What you really want is something like this."

She held up the box.

"A spirit casket. Warded with symbols imbued with the power, making it the perfect prison. I'll teach you the verse to expel Astaroth from Roland, and the words to bind him into the casket. Once he's inside, seal it. Then bury it. Deep. So deep it will never be found. And then, the world will never hear from Astaroth again."

Morgain taught me the verse and the words of binding, as well as the wards to shield our thoughts and plans from Astaroth's gaze. I wrote them all down before I began preparing to leave.

Once I was dressed again in my armor and weapons, Morgain took my hands in hers and looked me squarely in the eye.

"Promise me one thing, Maugis," she said, her voice suddenly soft. "Promise me you'll try to save her. I want to see my Angelica again, once she's free of Astaroth's poison."

I drew a breath, remembering the vow I'd made to Charles: to stop Angelica, even if it meant killing her. An oath I wished I had never spoken.

I looked into Morgain's eyes and saw the grief welling inside them.

"I'll save her," I said. "I swear it."

~

THE FINAL FAVOR Morgain did for me was waking Bradamante from her arcane slumber.

"What happened?" she murmured, rubbing her eyes as I led her through the misty veil back into the waking world.

"We were never going to match one of the Fae," I said. "They've walked the world for thousands of years. The ancients thought them gods. You managed to make her angry. Fortunately, all she did was put you to sleep."

Bradamante blinked at me. "And what did she do to you?"

"That's a long story. And one you need to hear. But first, let's find the horses."

We found Bayard and her charger where we'd left them. Once we were riding down the shepherd's trail, I told her everything I had learned about Roland in the spirit realm. As I spoke, I saw her hands tighten on the reins, her jaw hardening with each detail.

"She'll pay for that," she said when I finished, with no hint of sympathy for the notion that Astaroth's corruption might explain Angelica's actions.

"What now?" she asked.

I told her what Morgain had taught me about expelling and binding demons, and I showed her the spirit casket. We spent the rest of the ride shaping a plan to use it against Astaroth and free Roland. By the time the sun crested the hills, we knew exactly what we had to do. No matter how dangerous it would be.

I should have been exhausted after the long night, but I felt strangely alert, as if my body had been resting in a deep sleep while my spirit traveled the astral plane. Bradamante seemed equally refreshed. Though in her case, she had spent the entire night asleep under Morgain's spell.

When we reached the camp, the air still stank of smoke

from the burned watchtowers. Blackened canvas sagged where tents had stood, and soot streaked those that remained. Hoofprints tore the earth into churned ruts, and dark patches marked where blood had soaked the ground the night before. The camp looked less like an army's refuge and more like a field left behind by war.

After we stabled the horses, I headed for Turpin's tent while Bradamante went to gather the other paladins. The flap to the archbishop's tent was open. Turpin sat hunched in a chair, leafing through a worn prayer book beside an oil lamp. He looked up, and when he saw me, he sprang to his feet.

"Was it Morgain?" he asked.

"Yes." I stepped inside, my gaze flicking over the space. There was plenty of room to draw the symbol Morgain had taught me. "I know what she did to Roland. I felt her summon it, that hiss in the wind I sensed back in Verona. That was the moment."

Turpin raised a thick eyebrow. "Summon what?"

"A rather ancient demon lord," I said, "Astaroth, the Grand Duke of Hell. And I fear he's been spying on us through the spirit realm, hearing every word we've spoken with the king. I mean to put a stop to it."

Turpin's face paled. "A grand duke of hell?"

"*The* Grand Duke," I said. "Second son of the Dragon himself. He knows Orionde wants Charles to build an empire, and he means to destroy that future. It's only a matter of time before he uses Roland to strike at the King."

The archbishop swallowed hard, color draining from his cheeks. "Did Morgain tell you how to stop him?"

"She did. And we'll soon see if her methods work."

I pulled my book from its satchel and opened it to her instructions. Drawing my leaf-shaped blade, I knelt and pressed its tip to the carpet. I began carving a circle wide enough to touch each side of the tent, murmuring the incantation exactly as Morgain had taught me. Blue light bled from my sword's tip like ink from a quill, seeping into the ground. Within the circle, I traced a seven-pointed star, each tip touching the edge.

When the final word left my lips, the entire symbol flared with blue fire before fading from sight. The air inside the circle hummed with unseen force.

"Will that be enough?" Turpin whispered, eyes wide with awe.

"I hope so," I said. Though I could sense it: the ward had held.

A moment later, Charles strode into the tent, his gaze locking on mine with a glimmer of hope. Behind him came Bradamante, followed by Renaud, Olivier, and Guichard. Huon of Bordeaux brought up the rear, his face still pale and gaunt but no longer fevered. The plague of rats hadn't claimed him, and that alone was reason enough for hope.

"Tell me you have a plan to save Roland," Charles said.

"I do, Your Highness."

"Then let's hear it."

I told them everything I had revealed to Bradamante on our ride from the grotto. Charles's expression darkened when he heard of Roland's demonic possession, but eased slightly when I produced the spirit casket and explained how Morgain had taught me to expel and bind a demon. The others listened in silence, their faces a mixture of concern, awe, and unease.

When I'd finished, Bradamante and I laid out the plan we had forged on the trail. A plan that would take us back into the city, into the heart of the enemy's fortress, and face-to-face with Astaroth himself.

Charles nodded his approval when we finished. Olivier and Renaud were both enthusiastic about the boldness of the daring mission we had outlined, and Huon seemed pleased with the role he would play in it. Guichard, however, looked queasy at the thought of confronting a demon, unable to summon even one of his infamous quips. Turpin remained grave.

"I don't question this plan," the archbishop said. "I can think of none better. But I fear the mission's stakes are higher than we first suspected. If the demon's only aim were to stop our King, he could return in Roland's form, claim to have escaped, and strike Charles down in this very tent. But that would brand Roland a kingkiller and an outcast, hardly the useful vessel he is now.

"Instead, I believe Astaroth means to break us. To defeat the army of King Charles and replace his kingdom with another. One he would rule from the shadows, along with Angelica, who has already turned Desiderius and Adalgis into her unwitting pawns. Once he holds Francia, the rest of Christendom will fall. That's how the Devil takes back a world he once sought to rule."

A chill ran through my veins. Morgain had warned me as much, and now I understood. Astaroth was born to believe he was a god, destined to rule the mortal world.

Charles lifted his chin, fire in his eyes.

"I dare say," he announced, "it appears you fight for more than a king, and more than a kingdom. This is no longer a mortal contest, but a battle between Heaven and Hell. So today, I believe, you fight on the side of God and His saints. You fight to save our world."

His gaze swept over us as he drew Joyeuse, the steel gleaming in the lamplight. He held the blade high.

"For God and for Francia!"

CHAPTER 21

THE FORTRESS

A key to our plan was Father Laurent.

He had promised we could again use the old Roman drainage tunnel that led to the plague pit beneath the church of San Michele in Angusto, so long as we came in the service of the Pope. And tonight we did, in ways neither of us could have imagined just nights ago.

Pre-dusk fog rose off the Adige, and I thickened it with a few words of power uttered over my pewter chalice. As the sun sank in the west and frogs began their chorus along the riverbank, we rowed upstream in two boats, veiled by the fog. This time, Olivier, Bradamante, Renaud, and Guichard had left their shields at camp and draped old riding cloaks over their armor. We would need to slip through Verona's streets to reach the fortress, and shields would mark us as warriors. I, too, left my shield behind for my blackened staff, wearing a drab cloak over my mail. Ten minutes behind, in a second line of boats, Huon of Bordeaux followed with twenty of the King's best chevaliers and men-at-arms.

We found the rusted grate to the drainage tunnel loose,

just as we had left it. I slipped through first into the cramped, dank passage, the stench of rot clinging to the damp stone. My soul light flared to guide us, glinting off the trickle of black water underfoot, until we reached the entrance to the plague pit. There, I let the light die, conserving my strength for whatever waited above. For a moment, darkness closed in, then Guichard drew a torch from the sack over his shoulder and struck flint to steel. The flame leapt, throwing the mounds of bones and skulls into a hellish glow as we followed him through the maze of the dead toward the stairwell that climbed to the church.

From the stairway, we stepped quietly into the church's chancel, emerging behind the altar. Candlelight flickered from the shrines along the transepts and nave, as if someone had been keeping vigil here through the night. In the shadow of one shrine, a robed man knelt in prayer.

"Father?" I called softly.

The man turned toward us and rose. When the candle-light caught his eyes, I exhaled in relief. It was Father Laurent.

"I trust you haven't come seeking sanctuary this time?" Father Laurent asked, his slight frame silhouetted in the shrine's candlelight.

"No," I said. "Tonight we've come to save Verona."

His brows lifted. "Just the five of you?"

"Not quite. Within the half hour, Count Huon of Bordeaux will enter this church from the plague pit with twenty men. Their task is to take the city gates and open them to our King and his cavalry. Charles comes in peace. He has forbidden looting, and any man who tries to take a woman of Verona by force will lose his head."

Laurent blanched and made the sign of the cross. "I pray your men obey their king."

"Only the greatest of fools would test the word of King Charles of Francia," Olivier said.

The priest nodded with a hint of resignation, then spread his hands. "And you?"

"Our business lies in the Prince's fortress," I told him.

Bradamante's jaw tightened. "We mean to put a stop to the Prince's witch, once and for all." The edge in her voice sent a chill up my neck.

Father Laurent swallowed hard. "Well, then …"

"Do you know how well the fortress will be defended?" Renaud asked.

Father Laurent considered this. "The prince is a soft man, more devoted to his pleasures than to war. I doubt he expects an assault on his palace atop the hill, not while your King's army sits more than a quarter mile outside the walls. He also has a new champion, one of your King's commanders who has turned sides. You've seen the raids. To hear the prince's partisans tell it, they've been so effective that the siege may be broken in days. I imagine the prince sleeps quite comfortably in his palace tonight."

"Any chance he leaves the fortress gates open?" Guichard asked, a trace of hope in his voice.

Laurent shrugged. "That I cannot say. But there is a small postern door in the east wall, near the palace. The old Lombard kings used it to smuggle their mistresses in and out, away from jealous eyes."

My companions and I traded surprised glances. Guichard's sack held rope and grapple for scaling the walls, but slipping through a hidden door was far less perilous.

"The door will be locked, of course," Father Laurent added.

I allowed myself a thin smile. "That won't be a problem."

Father Laurent sent us off with a prayer, and we

departed the church to begin our trek toward the fortress. We knew that the raiding parties struck in the hours before midnight, but preparation for those sorties would have begun much earlier. Which meant our time to catch Astaroth before he set the night's plans in motion was already short.

Outside, the streets were nearly empty in the hush of night, fear of the siege keeping most behind barred doors. We kept to the shadows, threading narrow alleyways and steering clear of the pools of light cast by the lanterns that swung above the broader avenues.

We rounded the arena, its looming arches blotting out the stars, and ducked down another street. Relief washed over me when I saw that the gateway through the old Roman walls stood open. But then I spotted the two guards leaning against the archway, spears in hand, talking quietly in the lantern light. One glanced our way, perhaps hearing the scrape of a boot on stone. We drew back into the alley, holding our breath until the men turned back to their conversation.

"We can kill them," Olivier muttered.

"Do we *always* have to kill them?" I whispered back. "Let me try it my way."

Olivier gave me a wry smile. "Be my guest. But if you fail, I'll kill them."

I nodded. Olivier wasn't cruel, only practical. Still, I was confident my plan would work.

I summoned my soul light into the crystal set in my ring, then hid my hand beneath my cloak. Hunching over, I shuffled from the alley with a limp, tapping my staff against the cobblestones and dragging my left leg behind me. I hoped the guards might view me as a cripple or a drunk, or both.

"Good evening," I slurred as I drew closer.

The scar-faced guard squinted. "No beggars allowed in the old city."

"Beggar?" I protested. "My sister lives inside."

The second guard puffed out his chest and stepped forward, close enough that I caught the sour stink of his breath.

"I don't care," the scarred man growled. He jabbed a finger toward my chest, and in that instant, I snapped my hand free and spoke a word of power. Soul light lanced from my ring into his eyes.

He cried out, clutching his face. I spun, driving my staff into the other guard's forehead with a sharp crack. He crumpled to the stones. Then I reversed the staff and drove the butt hard into the blinded man's temple. His head smacked against the archway before his knees buckled and he collapsed unconscious.

Olivier, Bradamante, and my cousins hurried from the alley into the gateway.

"Not bad," Olivier said with a grin. "But I'd still have killed them."

Renaud and Guichard dragged the unconscious guardsmen into the darkness behind the old wall, and we started up the winding street that climbed toward the fortress. The silhouettes of a handful of men moved atop its walls, so we crept beneath the shadows of the cypress trees lining the path.

As the fortress loomed closer, I saw the gates were closed, and gave silent thanks for Father Laurent's tip about the postern door. Above us, guards paced the battlements twenty feet high, their lanterns flickering against the stone. I counted six at most, far too few to cover the whole wall. We waited until the sentries on the eastern side turned their backs, then hurried to the base. The battlements jutted two feet beyond the wall, hiding us from view.

We shuffled along the wall until we found the postern door. Made of sturdy oak, the door did not budge when Renaud pushed on it. "Bolted shut."

"Not a problem," I said.

I summoned my soul light and pressed my palm into the door's stone frame, right where an iron bolt should have slid into the wall. I uttered words of power until the stone began to glisten, and what had been solid rock took on the texture of wet clay. I shoved against the door and felt the bolt slide through the wall as if it were sludge. With a faint creak, the door cracked open.

Voices drifted from the courtyard.

I peered through the crack.

Halfway between the stables and the palace, Roland stood in a tunic and breeches with Durendal belted at his hip. To my surprise, he was speaking with Adalgis. The prince, portly and overdressed in a gold-trimmed cloak and fine silks, looked almost ridiculous beside Roland's towering frame. Four guards with spears flanked the Prince, their mail glinting in the lantern glow, while nearby, grooms and half a dozen chevaliers tightened leather barding on restless warhorses. The snorts of stallions and the clink of harnesses carried across the yard.

"Tell me, Lord Roland," Adalgis said, pressing a fist into his palm, "that tonight is the night you break them!"

"Everything will come in time, my prince," Roland answered coldly, his voice not quite his own.

"But why not *now*?" Adalgis spread his hands, his tone nasal and insistent. "Kill a few of his paladins. That will send my brother-in-law scurrying back to Pavia. Once he's gone, I can rally the lords of Lombardy and break the siege of my father's city as well!"

Behind me, I heard Olivier huff and slide his sword from its scabbard.

"Remember the plan," I growled under my breath. "I need the demon's undivided attention, and I won't get that during a prolonged battle in this courtyard. As soon as we strike, lure him into the tower. I'll head there before you, where I'll be waiting at the top, with this." I patted the belt pouch containing the spirit casket, earning grim nods from my companions.

I glanced at Guichard. "While Renaud and Olivier are engaging Roland, don't forget to set fire to the stables. That will be Huon's cue to take the gatehouse."

"Right." He pulled a torch from his sack and struck flint against steel. Sparks flew, and in a breath the pitch caught, the flame flaring bright before settling into a steady burn.

I turned to Bradamante, meeting her gaze. "Make sure I get inside the tower."

"And if we cross paths with your witch?" she asked.

My stomach clenched. "Then one of us will deal with her."

CHAPTER 22

A DANCE OF SWORDS

The element of surprise was our greatest advantage, and when we struck, the courtyard erupted into chaos.

Adalgis's eyes went wide. He squealed, and two of his guards seized him, dragging him toward the palace. One of his spearmen lunged at Olivier, who batted the shaft aside, spun, and drove his sword through mail and into the man's ribs. The second guard froze a moment too long, giving Bradamante time to slice her blade across his throat beneath the rim of his helmet.

Behind them, the grooms and chevaliers cried out with a mix of fear and surprise. None of them wore armor, but the chevaliers had swords, and several drew theirs. The only man who didn't react with panic or surprise was Roland. Even over the din, I could hear the scrape of steel when he ripped Durandal from its scabbard. His smoldering gaze fixed on me a heartbeat before Renaud was upon him, their blades colliding in a ring of steel that echoed through the courtyard.

I caught a whiff of smoke and glanced to my right. Guichard had flung his torch into a bale of hay, scattering the grooms and sending the stallions into a frenzy. Hooves struck stone, whinnies pierced the air. A chevalier charged Guichard, but before I could see more, two others rushed me. Olivier met the first, parrying the man's strike with his sword and driving a dirk with his other hand into the man's gut. Bradamante caught the second chevalier's sword and shoved him back.

"Get to the tower!" she yelled.

The tower's door stood thirty yards away. My heart pounded as I darted towards it, only to flinch as an arrow whistled past my ear. Another thudded into the earth at my feet. I swore under my breath; I'd forgotten about the men on the walls. The two archers atop the battlements reached for more arrows while a half-dozen more were stringing bows or hurrying to join them. I would not make it to the tower before those archers could take another shot, so I ran into the melee, hoping they'd hold their fire rather than strike their own.

A chevalier barreled toward me, his blade hammering against mine. Pain jolted down my arm with the force of his blows. He raised his sword for the kill, but then Olivier's steel flashed, shearing the man's arm above the elbow. The chevalier shrieked, clutching his stump, before Olivier rammed a dirk through the back of his neck.

"Hold them off," I shouted as another chevalier rushed toward us.

As Olivier engaged the man, I glanced left where Renaud and Roland fought, steel ringing with their dance of swords. Roland may have been the greatest warrior in Francia, but my cousin was nearly his equal, and for now, he was holding his own. To my right, horses shrieked as Guichard, aided by a pack of young grooms, flung open stalls and drove beasts from the burning stables, adding fresh mayhem to the courtyard.

That gave me a heartbeat to deal with the archers. I spun my sword, uttering the words to summon the wind. The air sizzled, then a gale roared from my blade, smashing the battlements. Archers reeled, arrows torn from their strings, helmets ripped from their heads. I prepared to sprint toward the tower door when fire seared my neck. The blaze that had begun with Guichard's torch now writhed unnaturally across the stable's frame, twisting like a nest of vipers. Flames raced along the thatch roof in streaks of eldritch blue, and a jet of fire shot toward me. The fire caught my cloak, so I ripped off the brooch and let the cloak fall, consumed by the unnaturally swift flames. I rushed out of the burning stable.

And that's when I saw her.

High on the tower's balcony stood Angelica, moving her blackened staff in patterns that controlled the fire like a puppeteer pulling strings on a doll. She caught my eye across the courtyard and smiled, slow and cruel, as if she had been waiting for this moment. The flames danced higher, writhing and twisting as though they shared her delight.

Above the stables, the flames coiled into a vast serpent, rearing before it struck like a cobra. I thrust up my staff, shouting a word of power as the blaze descended. Heat surged through me, into the staff, and the torrent split around its point as though I had driven it into a waterfall. Fire sprayed to either side, scorching the air but sparing my flesh. For an instant, the inferno bent to my will, yet I felt Angelica's grip on it, her strength dragging against mine, threatening to wrench the flames back under her command. She had far more fire at her disposal than I did, and I knew that gave her the advantage in this tug-of-war.

Sweat stung my eyes as I ground my teeth against the strain. Then a blur crossed my vision: Bradamante, sprinting for the tower steps, sword high, her face contorted with rage.

"Enough, you bloody whore!" she screamed.

Angelica's concentration wavered, and with a serpentine hiss, the fiery arc collapsed, its coils unraveling into sparks and smoke.

Bradamante vanished through the tower door as Olivier's voice rang out behind me.

"Maugis, go!"

I risked a glance back. Roland's chest heaved, his face burning red with rage. Renaud had broken away and was sprinting for the tower.

I was closer. I lunged for the doorway and slipped inside just ahead of him.

"Go, go!" Renaud shouted.

Behind him, Roland's roar shook the courtyard as he thundered after us, closing the distance with every stride.

CHAPTER 23

BLACK WINGS AND A BLACK FATE

I raced up the tower's stairwell. On the landing, a door stood open to Angelica's chamber, and every instinct told me to go inside. Without a doubt, Bradamante had made it there first. But the pounding of boots behind me echoed like thunder through the stairwell, and Renaud's cry drove me on.

"Maugis, hurry!"

I clenched my jaw and forced myself to follow the plan, taking the second staircase that spiraled toward the top. My heart hammered as I bounded upward, then a scream tore the air from below—a woman's scream.

I could not tell if it was Angelica's or Bradamante's.

And I had no time to find out. Renaud was right behind me, his face taut with urgency.

When I reached the top of the stairs, I threw the door open. A rush of cold night air swept in, heavy with the stench of bird droppings and rotting straw. I stepped onto the tower's roof, lit by two lanterns swaying on posts in the breeze. A stone parapet ringed the platform, which was choked with the massive rookery. Wooden cages rose in

clusters, stacked one atop another like a ramshackle tene-
ment, their roosting bars crammed with rooks, crows, and
ravens. At the sight of me, they erupted in a chorus of
harsh caws.

Renaud barreled through the doorway after me,
forcing me to jump aside or be bowled over. The reason for
his haste came an instant later: the flash of Durendal,
whistling through the air in a blow meant to take off his
head. Renaud twisted clear, but the blade sheared through
his cloak and smashed against one of the lanterns. Burning
oil sprayed and caught fire; flames licked across the
wooden cages. Roland stormed onto the roof, his next
strike colliding with Renaud's parry in a sharp clang that
split the night and sent the panicked birds shrieking into a
frenzy.

Renaud strained against Roland's blade, teeth
clenched, every muscle trembling. With a guttural snarl,
Roland lashed out with his free hand, ripping the door
from a cage. Black feathers exploded into the air as a raven
flew into Renaud's face. He reeled, arms flailing, then
toppled hard onto the stone, his sword skittering out of
reach.

My breath caught.

Roland dipped low and brought Durendal down in a
killing stroke. Renaud rolled, but too late. The tip raked
across his back, slicing through chain and leather, spraying
blood across the stones.

I did the only thing I could to save him. Gripping my
quarterstaff in both hands, I swung with all my strength.
The crack of wood on bone rang out, and Roland staggered backward, dazed.

All around us, the rookery erupted. Birds shrieked and
flapped their wings; others burst free from their burning
cages, filling the air with smoke and feathers.

I let my staff fall and reached for the spirit casket, forcing the verse Morgain had taught me to the tip of my tongue.

Roland's gaze fixed on me, not the casket, with a fiendish grin splitting his face.

"Both of you will die here," he said, his voice like cold iron.

"Not before I send you back to Hell—*Astaroth!*" I spoke his true name, and the verse poured from my lips.

Roland froze. Durendal slipped from his fingers as coils of blue fire hissed across the parapet. Power surged through me, hot and electric, as the binding closed in. His face twisted, fury warring with terror, as a ghostly double shimmered over his flesh: Astaroth's spectral form, half-seen, layered atop my friend's body.

I raised my voice, each word of Morgain's verse striking like a hammer.

"Astaroth, spawn of Samyaza, by the power of the Fae and the angels, your masters in heaven, I bind you!"

The eldritch flames rippled over him. A groan rumbled from his throat. "No…"

I needed one final word to seal the binding. I drew it to my tongue.

Then the world exploded.

A windblast slammed into me with the force of a tempest, ripping the casket from my hands and hurling it over the parapet. I staggered, cloak whipping, as Angelica burst from the stairwell, gripping her leaf-shaped blade. The flames around Roland's form guttered, flickering like a dying candle.

My mind reeled, clutching at one desperate thought.

The tale of the swine—Morgain told me another way to trap a demon.

I adjusted my verse and spoke the final words, ending

with the one to seal the binding. The air pulsed. The blue flames surrounding Roland flared, followed by an agonizing wail as the demon's spirit tore from his mortal vessel and streamed with the blue fire into one of the screeching ravens.

Angelica screamed. "What did you do?"

The horror in her eyes hardened into fury. She charged, shrieking, her sword raised to cut me down. I spun, my arm colliding with hers, knocking her strike astray. Momentum carried her into the parapet.

Then over it.

"No!" I lunged, grasping for her hand, but caught only air. Her scream trailed into the night as she plunged onto the burning thatch below. Fire swallowed her; a heartbeat later, the roof caved with a thunderous crack, and the stables erupted into an inferno.

"Angelica!" The cry tore from my chest. Smoke stung my eyes as I choked back a sob.

Then the bells began to ring, dozens of them, mingling with the blare of warhorns. From the tower, I saw torchlight flood Verona as the King's cavalry charged through the open gates.

Beside me, Renaud groaned, dragging himself upright. "You did it."

I stared at him, hollow inside. "I killed her."

Renaud shook his head. "No, cousin. You saved us— and you saved him."

Roland knelt on the stone floor, clutching his head, a low moan slipping from his lips.

Still, the words would not leave me. "I killed her."

"She damned herself," Renaud said softly, laying a hand on my shoulder. "When she fell for that demon."

I looked up. A dark storm of wings circled the tower, crows and ravens wheeling in the firelight. I wondered which one held Astaroth's spirit, trapped in its new vessel. Yet did it even matter? What could he possibly do as a crow?

My thoughts returned to the present when Guichard burst through the doorway, his face pale, streaked with sweat and soot. He glanced at Roland, then at his brother and me.

"Is it over?" he asked.

"Yes, brother," Renaud said.

Guichard gave a tight nod, but his expression darkened. "Maugis …" His voice cracked. "You have to come fast. It's Bradamante … she's dying."

GUICHARD LED me down the stairs to Angelica's chambers. Inside, we found Bradamante slumped in Olivier's arms, her fingers clutched around his hand. Her face, bathed in the light from a nearby oil lamp, was as pale as I'd ever seen it.

My gaze slid downward, reluctant, until it found what I dreaded most. The hilt of a dagger jutted from her chest, two inches above her heart. A chill seeped into my bones.

Bradamante looked up at me, wincing as she tried to laugh.

"She hit me with her bloody soul light." Her voice was weak. "So, bright … blinded me. I didn't even see it when she stuck me."

I felt a sudden weight on my chest. I'd never healed a wound this grave. I didn't even know if it was possible. But one thought gave me a sliver of hope. The blade had missed her heart, or she'd already be dead.

"You can save her, right?" Olivier asked, his gaze desperate.

"Yes," I said, though I didn't know if it was the truth or a lie.

I knelt down beside her. Bradamante looked up at me. I could see the fear in her hazel eyes. She was the bravest woman I'd ever known, as brave as Roland and Renaud. Perhaps even more so. But I suppose even the most courageous person feels fear when standing on the threshold of death's door.

From behind me came the sharp intake of breath.

I turned. Renaud stood there with his arm around Roland, who still looked dazed. Blood ran down Renaud's leg, a dark stain spreading from the gash in his back. That would need healing, too, but I was running out of time to save Bradamante.

I fixed my gaze on Olivier. "On my word, you need to pull out that dagger. Do it fast. I'll do the rest."

Bradamante groaned.

Guichard dropped to one knee, taking her free hand and holding it tight.

I drew in a deep breath, clearing my mind, then pressed my ring to my lips. I whispered the word into the crystal. *"Eoh."*

A halo of white light burst forth, settling into a steady glow. I brought it close to the dagger's hilt.

"Now," I told Olivier.

Bradamante cried out as he slid the knife free.

Blood gushed from the wound, but I clamped my hand over it, bathing it in soul light. I began reciting the words, imagining her skin, her muscles, her veins, willing them whole again. When I reached the end of the verse, I spoke it once more. Then again. Blood stopped oozing through my fingers, and I felt the power seeping into the gash, drawing the torn muscle together.

I could feel her heartbeat beneath my palm, her chest

rising and falling with each breath. My own breathing matched the rhythm of hers, as the power pulsed inside her with each spoken word. A growing warmth surrounded my hand, and in the light, I saw color returning to her face. She drew a deep breath, and I sensed it was done. The wound had healed.

She gazed up at me, the fear gone from her eyes. I slipped an arm around her shoulders and lifted her close.

"You're going to be alright," I said, feeling her breath against my skin.

"Thank you," she whispered. Her bottom lip brushed the top of mine.

In that moment, I wanted to stay there and kiss her. To lose myself in something other than Angelica.

But then warhorns blared outside the tower. I released her into Olivier's arms.

"The King has arrived!" Guichard exclaimed.

"Let's not keep him waiting long," I said. "But first, Renaud, take off your coat and show me your back."

BY THE TIME I finished healing Renaud, the cost of wielding so much power left me hollow and weak. Whatever strength I'd clung to was gone, leaving my legs too weak to hold me until Guichard hauled me to my feet.

Olivier, still the hardiest among us, had already gone down to greet Charles in the courtyard and report our success. Bradamante and Renaud, though no longer bleeding, moved stiffly. A brush with death always left its mark, no matter how well the flesh was mended.

Roland, perhaps the strongest of us in body, slumped against the wall of Angelica's chamber, one hand pressed to his brow. His gaze was unfocused. "What happened?" he muttered. "I was captured, then …" He shook his head.

"Let's just say you were not yourself these past few days," Renaud said. "But you're better now, thanks to Maugis."

We left the tower, walking gingerly, my arm around Guichard's shoulders. The courtyard blazed with torchlight, gleaming off the armor of scores of our chevaliers and men-at-arms. Charles's banners rippled in the night wind, their shadows spilling across the curtain wall. The Oriflamme stood among them. Judging by the number of the prince's men laying down their swords, their surrender was complete.

I should have felt triumph. Instead, the crackle of embers drew my eyes to the stables. They lay in ruins, thatch and timber still spitting smoke and flame. My stomach clenched at the thought of Angelica buried beneath that smoldering wreck. A tightness seized my chest, and I could not look away until a familiar voice broke through.

Turpin came striding toward us, his face beaming. "By God and good Saint Denis, Maugis, you did it!"

I managed only a vacant nod as Guichard let me go. Then Turpin's arms closed around me in a bear-like embrace.

"You did it," he said again, pride in every word.

"I did," I whispered, grief coiling through me. "I killed her."

PART THREE
THE ONCE AND FUTURE KING

CHAPTER 24

THE QUEEN AND THE PAWN

"I killed her."

The words tumbled from Maugis' lips in choking sobs.

"I killed Angelica."

He hung in the silvery-white web, chest heaving. Around him, the Lethe spiders watched with their cold black eyes.

"Poor Maugis," Nimue said, rising to her feet, her skin like frost. "So terribly tragic. She *never* would have found that book without you."

She let out a quiet laugh.

"And *that* book, of all things. You handed her a conduit to Astaroth himself. What did you think was going to happen?"

Maugis pressed his eyes closed. The pain felt as real now as it had back then.

"Perhaps you were ignorant of his purpose," she went on. "Though I dare say the title—the *Book of Shadows*—should have given it away. But once it was in her hands, it was too late. He plucked at her mind like a harp, every note sinking deeper, until all she wanted was the touch of his hands on her skin."

Maugis's skull pounded as memory surged. The tower ... Angelica and Roland entwined in passion, while the demon's translucent form pressed over Roland's body, as if he too shared their embrace.

"Stop ..." Maugis pleaded.

"She desired nothing more than to bring her new lover into the world and surrender herself completely, in mind, in body. And look how close she came." Nimue's tone carried a hint of admiration. "Together, they might have ruled all of Europe. From the shadows, perhaps, but Astaroth thrives in darkness. Yet you ended that, didn't you?"

Her eyes narrowed. "When you threw her into the flames."

A groan escaped him.

"Did you watch her burn?"

"Stop," he growled through clenched teeth.

"Did you hear her scream?"

His whole body trembled.

"Did you bury what was left of her?"

Maugis' eyes flew open. "What do you want from me?" he roared.

Nimue frowned, unmoved by his anger. Then a cruel, thin smile spread across her lips.

"I want you to suffer," she said. Her voice was as sharp as a blade. "I want to break you."

Maugis shook his head. "Why?" he muttered.

"Because I'm going to let you live. I'll send you back to Orionde a shattered man. So if she ever dares send another pawn against me ..."

Nimue bared her teeth. "She'll know exactly what will become of it."

CHAPTER 25

THE CRYSTAL CAVE

ours earlier, Bradamante had followed Merlin through the tunnels of Avalon. The walls glimmered with the faint, purplish glow of lichen, just enough light to guide Roland and Turpin as they trailed close behind, their footfalls echoing in the stone passageway.

She still didn't know if she could trust the man. Merlin had been furious when she woke him from his centuries-long sleep, and angrier still when he learned Orionde had enlisted the Franks. Yet he had healed her wounds, and since seeing Roland and Turpin and mistaking them for men he once knew, he seemed changed. Still mysterious, but no longer openly hostile.

Her doubts flared again when he veered right at one of the tunnel's many forks. "You're going the wrong way," she said.

He stopped, turning toward her with narrowed eyes. "Is this my old home or yours?"

"The way back to the lake is left," she snapped,

pointing down the opposite passage. "That's where she has Maugis."

"I'm sure he'll still be there when we return," Merlin replied.

Heat flushed her cheeks. "That's a chance I won't take. We need to save him now!"

Merlin's brow knitted into a scowl.

"What's the problem?" Roland called from behind.

"He's leading us away from Maugis," Bradamante said, her fists clenching at her sides.

Roland's gaze flicked to the wizard.

"Is she always this headstrong?" Merlin asked, more to Roland than to her.

Her mouth fell open. "I beg your pardon?"

Roland chewed his lip, trying not to grin. "Do you mean rash, impulsive, demanding at times? Then yes."

Fury boiled under her skin. She turned on her cousin, ready to strike him. "How dare you both!"

"Listen to me," Merlin said, his voice firm. "We are in no position to simply storm in and attack the Lady of the Lake. She was ancient when Atlantis sank beneath the sea. She ruled the Tuatha Dé Danann in their wars with the sons of Mil, long before Britain even had a name. By the time the giants raised their circles of stone, she was already old. And when gods themselves walked the earth, before the Flood swept their empires away, Nimue stood among them. So tell me, what do you expect will happen if we march up and demand she release your friend?"

Bradamante sucked in a sharp breath. Maugis had warned her once about another Fae, years ago, at the Fumane Grotto. *Morgain.* She still remembered how *that* turned out.

A gentle hand touched her shoulder. She glanced back to find Turpin.

"Perhaps we should listen to him," the archbishop said quietly.

"Fine," she huffed, glaring at Merlin. "So where exactly are we going?"

"If what you've told me is true," Merlin said, "I haven't eaten for several hundred years. And I refuse to face the battle of our lives on an empty stomach."

Bradamante blinked at him, dumbstruck, until she realized her own stomach was growling.

Roland shrugged. "He's not wrong. Everyone says, never go to war without a good breakfast."

Merlin nodded his solemn approval. "Precisely."

He led them through a warren of twisting tunnels until stopping before a circular wooden door bound in iron. Merlin pressed his palm to the wood. The hinges groaned as the door swung open, obedient as a hound. The chamber beyond lay in utter darkness.

Merlin whispered a few words, and a row of rushlights flared to life. Their glow revealed a stone-walled kitchen: a hearth large enough to roast an ox, blackened spits dangling from their hooks, along with hanging cauldrons. A trestle table and two benches stood coated in dust, as if no hand had touched them in an age.

"Now look at that," Roland grinned, "a kitchen."

"Don't mind the place," Merlin said dryly. "The Fae don't cook often."

Turpin glanced at Roland, raising an eyebrow.

Her cousin shrugged, then poked his head into one of the cauldrons. "Empty," he muttered.

Bradamante had disliked this detour, but the thought of food tugged at her, and her stomach betrayed her with a groan.

"No fear," said Merlin, his eyes glinting. "We didn't come for the kitchen. We came for the larder."

He crossed to another round door on the far wall. When he opened it, a waft of earth, mint, and sage spilled into the kitchen. Bradamante followed him into a large chamber lit by more flickering rushlights.

Inside, boxes of rich soil brimmed with green growth: the feathered tops of carrots, the broad leaves of cabbages and kale, the long stalks of leeks. Fronds of parsley and rosemary brushed against mint, thyme, and sorrel, while peas and beans wound their tendrils across wooden frames. The colors were startlingly fresh, even though sunlight had never touched them.

Turpin shook his head in wonder. "By God and good Saint Denis, how can anything grow down here with no sun?"

A spark of memory softened Merlin's eyes. "Cadoc asked the same question. I reminded him, we *are* in the Otherworld. But, if you must know, the stones on these walls and beneath those soil boxes are etched with sigils. You can only see them in the proper light, but they're imbued with the timeless power of the Fae to sustain life where nothing should grow. The enchantment also wards off blight and rot, so fortunately, nothing in here can spoil."

Bradamante breathed deeply, awed by the mingling scents of herbs and damp earth.

Merlin, meanwhile, was prying the lid off a nearby barrel. He dipped a ladle inside, sniffed, and slurped down a generous mouthful. For a heartbeat, Bradamante half-expected him to gag.

"Ah," he said, wiping a fleck of foam from his beard, "the ale's still good, after all these years."

Merlin thrust the ladle toward Roland. "Try some."

Roland took a swig, then another, before passing it to Bradamante with a satisfied grunt. She lifted it to her nose, half expecting the ale to smell sour. Instead, it was rich and heady, and when she drank, it slid smooth and warming down her throat.

She passed the ladle back to Roland, who offered it to Turpin, while Merlin rummaged through another barrel. From it, he drew a small bundle wrapped in cloth and handed it to her. She unwrapped it, revealing a small loaf of bread. She was certain the bread would be as hard as stone, but the loaf was soft beneath her fingers, its aroma rich with honey and butter. She took a bite and for a moment forgot herself entirely. It was heavenly, perhaps the best bread she had ever tasted.

"Take what you want," Merlin said, already reaching for another loaf. "We need to eat and get moving. We have plenty to do if we're going to save your friend."

Bradamante took a second loaf and plucked a carrot and a turnip from the dark brown soil. Turpin gathered a portion large enough for himself and Roland, while her cousin returned with one of the smaller cauldrons and began filling it with ale.

They ate quickly while fielding questions about the wine in Francia from Merlin, who was curious if they were still the finest in Europe. They enjoyed the ale, too, but not too much, after Roland reminded them of another of his warrior sayings. "Eat well, but never show up drunk for a fight."

When they left the kitchen, Bradamante expected Merlin to turn back the way they had come. Instead, he strode down another passage dimly lit by phosphorescent lichen.

"Where are we going now?" she asked, her annoyance creeping back despite the warmth of bread and ale in her stomach.

Merlin gave her a stern look. "If we're to have any

hope of stopping Nimue, I must first return to the Crystal Cave."

He strode off, and they followed. After a short walk, the tunnel bent left and ended at an iron-bound door. He seized the handle, and as the hinges groaned, a blinding white brilliance spilled into the passageway, forcing Bradamante to shield her eyes.

She blinked hard, then stepped to the threshold. And gasped.

The chamber beyond was a great circular hall, its walls sheathed in crystal. Columns of quartz jutted upward, casting silvery light that danced with veins of molten gold. Above, the ceiling soared thirty feet high, stalactites dripping with a pale glow like frozen moonlight. For an instant, she thought of Morgain's grotto in the hills above Verona, yet this place was different, alive with its own inner fire. And at its heart stood a chest-high pedestal of diamond-clear crystal, crowned with a silvery orb the size of a cabbage from Avalon's larder.

"By God and good Saint Denis," Turpin muttered.

Roland gave a low whistle. "Well, that's something."

"What is that?" Bradamante asked, her gaze fixed on the gleaming orb.

Merlin stepped to the pedestal, his hand hovering just above the surface. "A Seeing Stone," he said. "Think of it as a window into what has been. Not to all things, but to moments etched in fate. Deeds of passion and sorrow, of triumph and betrayal. The great turnings of the world, when men's choices shape the course of destiny."

"And what do you mean to do with it?" Bradamante pressed.

"I'm going to use it to search for a way to stop her." Merlin's left hand settled on the orb, and a soft silver light rippled through the stone. "Now, gather around. You'll all want to see this."

She stepped closer, and Merlin extended his hand toward her. She hesitated, then drew back.

"I must guide the Stone," he said, steady and calm. "But if you are to see what I see, we must all be joined, hand to hand."

Bradamante gave a slow nod. She placed her palm in his and offered her other to Roland. He clasped it firmly, then reached across to take Turpin's hand, completing the circle. She drew in a sharp breath as a faint thrum passed through their joined hands, setting her nerves on edge.

"Let us begin with the first moment you beheld Nimue," Merlin said. Then he spoke a verse in that alien tongue Maugis had used when he wielded the power.

With each syllable, light swelled within the Stone until it blazed like a tiny sun. Bradamante squinted, certain the brilliance would sear her eyes. But then, in a sudden burst, the glare softened, unfurling into the moonlight glow of Avalon's lake, where the great tree rose from the waters.

Bradamante's eyes widened. Four figures were approaching the great tree: herself, Turpin, Roland, and … Maugis. She watched them in awe, like some disembodied spirit hovering ten feet behind.

This was us. Earlier today.

Ahead, two silhouettes waited in the glow of the lake. One stood taller than the other, both swathed in black robes that seemed to drink the light. At their feet, three crouching shapes gleamed pale as bone.

The hounds …

She saw herself and the others halt and sink to their knees.

She remembered why. The man's voice had thundered: *Kneel before the Lady of the Lake!*

Within the Stone, however, no sound carried, as if hearing lay beyond its power. But she knew what came next.

And the dread of reliving it clenched hard in her chest.

CHAPTER 26

THE LAST ENCHANTMENT

Roland could hardly believe his eyes. He was staring at himself, not like through a silvered mirror, but as if he were some unseen ghost haunting his own steps.

How the Stone could show him what he had lived only hours before, he could not guess. Only that it was magic. And he had never trusted magic. He endured it only when Maugis bent it to their aid. Yet now, all he could do was pray that Merlin's motives proved as true as his friend's.

But there was no time to dwell on it. His gaze was fixed on the vision unfolding in the orb, and though he knew well what was about to happen, he could not look away.

On the shore, Roland watched Nimue draw back her cowl, her hair shimmering in the lake's silver glow. She was speaking, but no sound reached them from the orb. He remembered the words well enough: *Orionde has at last sent her lackeys to rob me of what is mine. Who among you is her apprentice?*

He saw Maugis rise to his feet. They spoke, or rather, she demanded his name, and he gave it. Roland recalled her cold reply: *What shall I do with you, Maugis d'Aygremont — Maugis the Thief — now that you've come uninvited into my realm?*

Maugis had drawn Orionde's letter from his satchel then, still speaking silent words. The cowled man at Nimue's side stepped forward, the younger one, dressed in Benedictine robes. The orb drew close upon his face: pale, gaunt, handsome.

Merlin tapped a deliberate pattern on the Stone's surface, and then the vision froze. His eyes narrowed. "So, Nimue has taken another lover." His gaze lingered on the frozen face. "Do you recall his name?"

"Eadric," Bradamante answered, unable to peel her eyes from the orb.

"What was in this letter?" Merlin asked.

"A symbol," she said. "A sigil, Maugis called it, one Orionde herself had drawn. He said it could stun Nimue, render her unconscious long enough for us to finish the mission."

"Hmm." Merlin tapped the Stone again, and the vision lurched back into motion.

Eadric broke the seal and unfolded the parchment. Horror flickered across his face as his skin flushed red, then blackened, smoke curling from his flesh as though he were burning alive from within.

Nimue's face twisted in fury. Eldritch blue fire leapt from her fingertips.

Roland felt Bradamante shudder beside him, her hand tightening in his.

Maugis threw back his head, his face contorted in agony. His body arched, clawing at the air as blue fire licked across his skin.

Roland saw himself cry out and lunge for his sword, only to be caught and held back by Turpin's strong grip.

He remembered the helpless rage in his chest, Turpin urging them to run.

Within the orb, he watched their flight replayed: himself, Turpin, and Bradamante fleeing into the dark, the three pale hounds bounding after them. The vision followed until they vanished into shadow, but the Stone's gaze did not pursue them.

Instead, it lingered, fixed on Maugis.

A cold prickle raced across Roland's skin. What came next was not memory, it was revelation.

He saw Maugis collapse, limp and lifeless, upon the ground. Nimue paused to look down on Eadric's smoldering remains, his flesh charred to coal. Then her gaze hardened. She strode to Maugis, bent down, and lifted him effortlessly into her arms, as though neither his weight nor his armor amounted to anything at all.

She bore him to the lakeshore and, bathed in the glow rising from the moonlit water, laid him in a narrow boat, its hull fashioned of stretched hide over a wooden frame. Nimue stepped in after him and rowed across to the island where the roots of the titanic tree rose like burial mounds heaped upon one another. At the far side, she lifted him once more and carried him up a stairway spiraling into the tree's stone-gray bark.

The orb's unblinking eye followed her climb, step after step, until she emerged at last onto a vast terrace built high among the branches. Broad as a great hall and paved in ancient stone, it offered space enough for a king's court to gather there. A crumbling balustrade, fissured with cracks, curved in a crescent around the platform, while the tree's colossal limbs jutted outward beyond the edge, their smaller branches twisting upward like skeletal claws against the sky.

She laid Maugis on the stone floor, then crouched

down and removed the satchel slung around his shoulder. She tossed it aside, then unbuckled his sword belt, tossing that as well, before pulling his mail hauberk over his head, followed by his gambeson, until only his sweat-stained tunic remained. Then she straightened, raising her hands toward the branches as blue fire flared at her fingertips. For a moment, nothing stirred. Then Roland saw them: spiders the size of a man's hand, hairless and white as bone, scuttling down from above. Five in all, moving with eerie precision, leaping branch to branch until they worked together to weave a web of glistening silver. In moments, it was finished, stretched wide enough to snare a man.

"What are those?" Turpin asked.

"Lethe spiders," Merlin replied grimly. "Among the deadliest creatures in the Otherworld."

Bradamante's grip tightened around Roland's hand. He clenched his jaw, trying to ignore the chill that crawled down his spine.

Nimue turned to an iron-bound door set into the tree's trunk. She spoke a silent command, and it opened.

Through the doorway lumbered a monstrosity unlike anything Roland had ever seen. When it straightened to its full height, it must have stood ten feet tall. Man-shaped, yet no man: its torso and limbs were hammered from black iron, joined by hinges at the elbows and knees. Its hands and feet were massive, each finger and toe a thick iron rod linked by more of those uncanny joints. Worst of all was its head, an iron skull with hollow sockets burning with smoldering blue fire.

Roland's stomach knotted as a second giant emerged behind the first. "What are those?"

"Golems," Merlin said bitterly, stilling the vision with a touch of his fingers upon the Stone. "These are forged of iron, but they can be made from flesh, even bone."

"A golem?" Turpin asked. "I recall the word from old Hebrew texts. Beings made of clay and imbued with life through a symbol, one of the true names of God, etched on its forehead."

"These are abominations of those holier creations," Merlin explained. "They are empty vessels until a sorcerer traps a spirit within them, twisting it into a slave. Such craft reeks of necromancy. I would never have thought Nimue capable. At least not until she loosed that undead drake upon us."

"Can they be killed?" Roland asked.

Merlin's gaze flicked to Durendal at Roland's hip. "Is that sword Fae-forged?"

Roland nodded. "The Fae of Rosefleur made it."

"Then yes," Merlin said simply.

Roland forced himself to look back into the Seeing Stone as Merlin touched the Stone, and the image sprang back to life. The two golems stooped, seized Maugis by the arms, and lifted him like a doll. They held him against the silver web while the spiders leapt to their work, spinning silk around his wrists and ankles, winding him tighter and tighter until he sagged, bound and unconscious.

Their task complete, the iron giants turned and lumbered back through the doorway, vanishing into the tree's heart. Nimue lingered. She stepped close, her pale arm stretching toward her captive, slender fingers seizing his chin. She tilted his face upward, studying him. Her gaze roved over every line of his features until his eyelids began to flutter.

Then the vision faded.

"We have seen enough," Merlin said. "Now we must journey deeper into the past, more than two centuries before this night."

His fingers traced their pattern across the orb, and the

light shifted. A forest came into view, its trees beaded with dew.

There stood Merlin, little changed from the man beside them now, cradling a young woman in his arms. She could not have seen more than twenty summers. Her raven hair, braided long, spilled down her sage-green dress. Her eyes closed as she kissed him. When she opened them again, wide with joy, Merlin smiled back at her, his silver mustache lifting with a warmth Roland had not yet seen on the wizard's face.

"Is that Sebile?" Bradamante asked softly.

Roland knew the name from Brother Meical's story.

Merlin's brow rose, sorrow gathering in his eyes. "Yes," he said, his voice cracking. "How did you know?"

"A monk from the abbey, Brother Meical, told us of you two. That you were lovers."

"We were," Merlin admitted. "She was my apprentice."

Roland watched as the young woman darted into the trees, only to return with a blackened staff clutched in her hands. It resembled Maugis', but it appeared heavier and more ominous. Strange symbols crawled along its length, carved into the ebony wood as if alive.

She offered it to Merlin. His face lit with awe as he accepted the staff. He spoke to her, words they could not hear through the orb, then he embraced her again, kissing her lips with fervor.

"The staff was her gift to me," Merlin murmured, eyes locked on the vision. "She called it *Lorg Mór*, the Great Staff. It had belonged to the Dagda himself."

"Dagda?" Turpin asked.

"In the old tales, he's a king among the Fae. In others, he's the first and mightiest of the druids. Sebile was of druid blood, her line reaching back to Éire. She was born with a gift for the power. But the staff she gave me ..." He shook his head, his gaze still fixed on the image. "Lorg Mór was power incarnate, a weapon older and more potent than anything I had ever wielded."

The image shifted.

Merlin was there again, but not alone. A woman's pale arms curled around his bare back as they moved together in a slow, fervent rhythm. His fingers tangled in long hair, not raven-black like Sebile's, but silverspun. When at last they parted, Nimue's face was revealed, flushed and heaving with breath.

Bradamante's expression darkened. "I thought Sebile was your lover."

"She was," Merlin said softly. "But we were at war with the Saxons, and Arthur needed Avalon's aid. As did I. So I gave Nimue what she wanted, hoping she would give us what we needed. I hid my love for Sebile, thinking Nimue would never know. But I was a fool ..."

The vision showed him rising from the bed, donning the same gray robes he now wore. Nimue's eyes hardened as she watched. Words passed between them, silent in the orb, until her gaze flared with fury. Merlin's face reddened in alarm.

She leapt from the bed, her hand outstretched. Blue fire erupted from her fingers. Merlin arched, mouth open in a scream they could not hear, his body clawing at the air. At that instant, he was Maugis, suffering the same terrible fate. His legs gave out, and he crumpled to the ground.

Nimue stepped toward him, her beauty terrible in its perfection, like some goddess hewn in marble from the ruins of Rome. She bent, gathered him into her arms as easily as she had carried Maugis, and the scene blurred.

The glow of the Lethe filled the orb. A small boat drifted across its waters, Nimue at the oars, Merlin's limp body lying in the prow. She guided the craft to a barren islet of rock and reeds. There she knelt, pressing her palms to the soil. Eldritch fire leapt from her fingers, setting the reeds ablaze. The ground heaved. Slowly, the earth rose and swelled into a mound, broad and tall, until it resembled a barrow.

Nimue smoothed its surface, then returned to the boat. She lifted Merlin's body, laid him atop the mound, and folded his hands upon his chest. Placing her palms over him, she chanted words none of them could hear. Blue light washed across his form, seeping into the mound until it ran down the sides like streams of blood.

When the spell ended, she turned to go. But then she paused, her gaze lingering on Merlin's still face. For a heartbeat, her expression softened, sorrow flickering in her eyes. Then it was gone. Coldness returned, and she walked away.

The vision dimmed to a dull glow.

"Where is it?" Merlin muttered, his voice filled with frustration. "What did you do with it? Why won't you show me?"

"What do you seek?" Bradamante pressed.

"My staff," he said. "I must know what she did with it."

"Surely it can be found another way," Turpin offered.

Merlin shook his head. "Perhaps I searched too far into the past. The answer lies elsewhere."

Roland caught the glimmer in the wizard's eyes.

"I should have known sooner ..." Merlin's voice trailed off as his fingers tapped the Stone. Its glow brightened.

"Where are we going?" Bradamante asked.

"To where it all ended," Merlin said, his voice grave.

"A vision I once saw in my dreams, though I was not there to witness it. The place where I foretold Arthur's son, Mordred, would betray his father. At a battle called Camlann."

CHAPTER 27

THE WICKED DAY

A thick fog filled the orb. As it thinned, Roland looked upon a battlefield strewn with corpses of men and horses. Mud churned red beneath broken lances and shattered shields. What had begun as a cavalry charge had collapsed into a desperate melee on foot. Britons and Saxons hacked at one another with swords and axes, their armor slick with blood.

At the center fought a tall, broad-shouldered warrior, swinging a massive broadsword. He hewed down a Saxon with brutal force, blood splattering his weathered face. Though older, the resemblance was unmistakable. He fought with Charles's fury.

Arthur.

Beside Roland, Merlin drew a sharp breath.

Two Saxons rushed Arthur, and he cut them both down. A bearded Briton roared silently nearby, his axe splitting skulls as he carved a path through the enemy. Roland knew that face. *Huon.*

As the battle raged, Roland saw more familiar faces.

Renaud, Olivier, Guichard. They fought like lords of war, and men died at their swords.

A horde of Saxons pressed toward Arthur. His men bled, faltered, and fell back to shield their king. Roland felt a thickness in his throat as he watched their armor darken with blood. An angry gash ran down Huon's cheek, but the wound only fueled his rage as he hammered his axe into a Saxon's chest.

Then another warrior burst into the fray, charging through the Saxons with savage force. Blood misted the air as his blade rose and fell, cleaving one man after another. His long hair flew wild, his beard unkempt, his eyes burning with a fire Roland knew too well.

His own eyes. His own face.

Roland's breath caught. Not him, it could not be. And yet it was, the man Merlin had named *Lancelot.* He fought with a prowess that filled Roland with pride. But the Saxons were too many. Roland's stomach clenched as a Saxon drove a shortsword into Lancelot's gut. Still, Lancelot fought, killing three more before the wound drained him. Blood bubbled from his lips. He staggered. Then Arthur was there, cutting a path to him, Huon at his side. Arthur fell to his knees, grief etched into his face, and caught the dying warrior in his arms. Lancelot's last breath left him in his king's embrace.

Roland's heart fluttered in his chest.

The vision turned, and another figure took focus: a youth of perhaps eighteen, fighting with the Saxons. His blond hair clung to his brow with sweat, his polished armor splattered with blood. His face bore hints of Charles. And Arthur.

"Mordred," Merlin whispered.

The boy fought with a feral rage, his spear striking

down Briton after Briton as three towering Saxons cleared his path. He drove straight for his father.

Father and son met amidst a ring of corpses. Mordred charged. Arthur raised his sword. The spear punched through the chainmail above Arthur's waist. The blow should have stopped any man, but not this one. He pushed the spear inward, roaring silently with pain or rage. Then Arthur drew back his broadsword and plunged it through Mordred's heart.

Breath hissed from Merlin's lips.

The scene blurred.

Crows feasted on the battlefield, though pockets of fighting remained. A handsome, young Briton with auburn hair swung his blade. He killed a Saxon, then spun to engage another. Five more fell to his sword before he reached Arthur. Huon was already there, kneeling by Arthur's side, but the King's eyes were closed. Death had taken him.

Bradamante's hand tightened in Roland's grip. Narrowing his eyes, Roland spotted the resemblance. The auburn hair, the fair features. The warrior could have been Bradamante's brother.

"Who is that?" she asked.

Merlin's gaze was heavy with sorrow. "Galahad," he said. "Lancelot's son. The other is Gawain."

A third man came to Arthur's side, a warrior with Olivier's face, though dirt and blood marred his handsomeness.

"Percival," Merlin murmured.

The three bore Arthur's body from the field. The image shifted, and Roland's breath caught at the sight of a place he knew.

The three warriors stood on the fog-draped shores of Glastonbury, Arthur's body wrapped in a blood-stained banner. The hill of the isle rose ghostlike beyond the lake. In Galahad's hand gleamed Arthur's sword.

Through the mist, a boat approached. A woman in white robes stood within it, tall, statuesque, her long hair spilling dark as obsidian over her shoulders.

Bradamante's grip tightened on Roland's hand. Her eyes flicked to him, knowing.

Merlin's lips shaped a single word. "Morgain."

The warriors greeted her with words the orb did not carry. Then Percival and Gawain lifted Arthur into the boat while Galahad offered Morgain the sword. She accepted it, and the boat drifted into the fog, vanishing.

The vision blurred and returned, this time to Avalon's shore. A hide-hulled craft was beached beneath the colossal tree, the lake's glow gilding its roots. Morgain stepped out, carrying Arthur and the sword. She pressed through a door carved into the tree's base, its surface etched with symbols: a circle containing a star, ringed by sigils Roland did not recognize.

The chamber within yawned vast as a cathedral's chancel, though heavy shadows veiled much of its depth. Morgain bore Arthur to a stone slab like a bier, laying him as if in a crypt. She whispered silent words, then rose and carried the sword deeper, toward a wooden rack.

Other weapons rested there: a spear, another blade … and a staff, thick and blackened, runes crawling its length.

"*Lorg Mór*," Merlin breathed, hope sharpening his voice. "They kept it with the sword."

Merlin pulled his hand from the orb, and its light guttered out. The strange thrum in the chamber faded with it. Roland released Turpin's hand, then Bradamante's, and flexed his fingers, as though shaking off a lingering chill.

Something inside him felt unsettled. *It's not every day you watch yourself die.* He set his jaw. *But that wasn't me. That was Lancelot.*

"What do we do now?" Bradamante asked.

Merlin's eyes burned with renewed fire, as if the memory of his staff had breathed life back into him.

"I will reclaim my staff," he said, his voice steady. "And we will find the weapon Orionde sent you to claim. Then, together, we will fight to save your friend Maugis."

CHAPTER 28

EXCALIBUR

Merlin led them back through the dim tunnels of Avalon. They passed the door to the kitchen, then reached a fork where he veered suddenly to the right. Bradamante glanced left, convinced they had gone that way before. But was she sure? The twisting passages all looked alike. The longer she lingered in them, the more the maze gnawed at her sense of direction.

"Where are we going now?" she asked.

"Down a shortcut," Merlin replied, a hint of annoyance in his voice.

The tunnel bent left, darker now, the glow of lichen thinning until only sparse patches remained. Ahead, something stirred. Bradamante caught Merlin's sleeve.

"Look!" she hissed.

Twenty yards down, two pairs of eyes gleamed red as embers.

A low growl rumbled through the dark. The shapes padded forward, pale, hairless beasts the size of wolfhounds, their claws scraping against the stone.

"Hounds of Annwn." Merlin spat the name like venom.

Behind her, Roland unsheathed Durendal, steel whispering from the scabbard. Bradamante reached instinctively for her sword, only to grasp empty air. A curse caught in her throat. She remembered her shattered blade, lost on the islands around Merlin's tomb.

Turpin moved past her, clutching his silver cross. "The last time, this was enough to drive one of them away."

Merlin glanced at the cross. "That's because the hounds are unholy creatures. I've no doubt it might work on one of them, yet not before the other attacks. But I have another way."

The hounds crept nearer, their movements low and deliberate, like hunters closing in. Bradamante drew the dagger from her belt, her heartbeat quickening, as Merlin brought forth his crystal.

He inhaled deeply. "*Eoh!*"

A blinding blast of soul light burst from his palm. Bradamante shielded her eyes as the hounds yelped and skidded across the stone. Another wave followed, brighter still, flooding the tunnel with searing brilliance.

As the glare faded, she heard the clatter of claws retreating down the passage. She blinked until her vision cleared. When it did, the hounds were gone.

"Truly amazing," Turpin said, awe in his voice. "The soul light has that power?"

The faintest smile touched Merlin's lips. "Cadoc was always curious too," he said. "The soul resides in all of us. But to draw upon the divine spark and wield it as a weapon, that demands knowledge of the language of creation itself. That knowledge *is* power, and that's what the beasts of the Otherworld fear."

Turpin scratched at his beard, nodding slowly as he weighed the words.

"Will they come back?" Bradamante asked. Her concern was less about arcane mysteries than the unwelcome thought of those claws raking again in the dark.

"Unlikely," Merlin said. "But I've no wish to linger here and test it."

Merlin led them through another stretch of twisting tunnels until they reached a curtain of mist barring the way. As Maugis had done before, Merlin summoned his soul light, and the veil shivered and parted.

They stepped out onto the lakeshore. The waters glowed with their familiar pale light, and from the island rose the colossal tree of Avalon. Its vast, leafless branches clawed hundreds of feet into the air, vanishing into the shadowed heights above. The lake's glow revealed balconies and parapets carved into its bark, as pale and rigid as stone. Stairs wound upward in dizzying spirals, climbing into the dark. Bradamante's gaze followed them, her stomach tightening. She could not see Maugis or the silver web that bound him. But she knew he was up there. And so was Nimue.

Bradamante's muscles tensed as they neared the lake. Out here, they were exposed. If Nimue saw them from some high perch, who knew what kind of hell she might loose upon them?

"Wait," Roland whispered.

He stooped beside something long and dark lying on the hard-packed earth. Lifting it, he turned the blackened shaft in his hands.

Maugis' staff.

Bradamante remembered now. He had laid it down when they knelt before Nimue and her servant Eadric. Roland took it with him.

At the water's edge, Bradamante nearly exhaled in relief until she noticed the ox-hide boat was moored on the far side of the roots, where they plunged into the glowing water.

"Now what do we do?" she asked.

"Take turns," Merlin replied. "We'll cross in pairs, once I summon it."

He drew a small tin cup from his robe, smaller even than Maugis' chalice, and knelt to dip it in the lake. Whispering an arcane verse, he tipped the water back, and ripples spread outward in widening rings. When they touched the distant boat, the craft lurched, as if seized by an unseen current, and drifted slowly toward them.

"You two first," Merlin said, nodding to Roland and Turpin.

Roland and the archbishop climbed aboard. Turpin's bulk nearly filled the little hull, but Roland took the oar and rowed them across in silence. When they disembarked, Merlin summoned the boat back with another ripple of water, then motioned for Bradamante to join him.

Merlin rowed them across the glowing lake. As the boat scraped onto the island's shore, Bradamante's breath hitched. She knew this place. The roots towering above them, the glow of the Lethe washing the stones. It was the same scene she had watched in the Seeing Stone, where Nimue had borne Maugis. And where Morgain had carried the body of King Arthur.

Merlin led the way, and Bradamante realized they were retracing Morgain's path, climbing over the mound-like roots until they reached the door set into the tree's base.

Up close, the carving loomed even larger: a circle enclosing a seven-pointed star, each tip pressed against the outer ring. Vaguely familiar symbols filled the space between. Yet what unsettled her was the door itself.

There was no handle and no lock. Nothing to hold or force.

"Don't fret," Merlin said. "I have the key."

He lifted his crystal, breathed upon it, and the stone flared with soul light. When he touched it to the carving, the light spilled outward, racing through the lines until the star and its circling runes gleamed with a pearlescent glow.

A soft click echoed from within the trunk. Merlin pressed his palm to the door, and it swung inward.

The light in Merlin's crystal dimmed to a soft glow as he stepped into the chamber. Bradamante followed, a rush of cool, dry air washing over her. The place felt as vast as a cathedral's chancel, and the air carried the scent of stone and dust. Beneath her feet, every flagstone bore a strange mark, spirals and runes that seemed to shift in the glow. The curved walls were carved with the same sigils, their lines disappearing into the shadows above.

Merlin advanced, his crystal casting back the dark, and she saw what the vision had not shown. Where once a stone slab had lain, now stood a sarcophagus, its lid carved with the likeness of a monarch in repose. Merlin stared at the carving, sorrow misting his eyes. "They built him a tomb fit for a king."

But Bradamante's gaze was drawn elsewhere. Beside the tomb rose a squat standing stone, like those she had seen in Saxony. And driven into its heart was a great sword. Its cross-guard flared broad and straight, its hilt crowned with a round pommel where a pale gemstone flickered faintly in Merlin's soul light.

"Is that ...?"

Merlin nodded. "Excalibur."

"A sword in a stone," Turpin muttered.

"Impressive," Roland said. He glanced down at Durendal's hilt, as if weighing one sword against the other.

Merlin turned to Bradamante. "Is this not what Orionde sent you for?"

"It is."

"Then go seize it."

She hesitated for a moment, wondering if she was worthy to take the weapon, particularly if everything Maugis had told her about it was true. But why not her? She took a step, then another. The blade's steel shimmered in the glow of Merlin's crystal. She reached for the hilt.

The scream of iron hinges split the air. A blur surged from the shadows.

The blow struck like a battering ram, knocking the breath from her chest. She flew backward, arms flailing, and hit the flagstones hard enough to send pain searing through her shoulder. Gasping, she looked up and saw it, gleaming in Merlin's soul light. A towering figure of black iron, ten feet tall, its joints groaning as it stepped forward. It loomed over her companions, its massive frame interposed between them and the sword in the stone.

Before she could rise, Roland tore Durendal from its scabbard and struck the golem's thigh. Sparks flared as steel screeched against enchanted iron. The monster did not even flinch. With a backhand strike, it hurled Roland across the chamber, slamming him against the stones near the entrance.

Turpin bellowed, charging with his mace. "By God and all the saints—"

The golem lunged faster than its size should have allowed. Its massive hand seized Turpin by the arm and shoulder and wrenched him off his feet. Turpin hammered its wrist again and again, each blow ringing like a church bell, but the grip only tightened. His cry of pain filled the chamber.

Merlin rushed to Bradamante, offering his free hand. "Up! Quickly, you must take the sword!"

She scrambled to her feet. Roland was already back in the fight, ducking beneath a massive swing and driving Durendal down on the golem's wrist. The Fae blade bit through the iron. With a grinding crunch, the hand fell away.

The golem stared at the stump in disbelief. Then the flames in its eyes flared. It flung Turpin aside like a rag doll.

Bradamante darted behind it. While Roland fought to keep its fury on him, she gripped Excalibur's hilt. The weapon was shockingly cold, thrumming in her hands. For an instant, it would not move. Then she heaved. The blade slid free with a shriek of steel against stone that rang through the chamber.

"Aim for its head and chest!" Merlin called.

She swung, but the giant twisted. Sparks burst as her blow glanced off its hip. The monster's massive hand lunged for her.

Roland roared. Springing off Arthur's sarcophagus, he drove Durendal two-handed into the golem's chest. Metal split, sparks flew, but the giant ripped him free, leaving the sword buried to the hilt. Its grip closed around him, squeezing until his face contorted in agony.

"Roland!" Bradamante cried.

She hurled herself forward, swinging at its ankle with all her strength. Excalibur sheared clean through. The leg buckled. With a shattering crash, the golem toppled onto its back. Though it still clutched her cousin, crushing him.

"The head!" Merlin shouted.

Bradamante raised Excalibur high. With a cry, she brought it down, the blade cleaving through iron as if through flesh. Sparks flared, blue fire spilled from the golem's eye sockets, and wisped into smoke. The head toppled from the neck, ringing across the flagstones.

Roland pried the golem's fingers from his shoulder one by one, each motion wringing a grimace of pain. At last, he dragged himself free, planted a boot on the giant's torso, and wrenched Durendal from its iron chest.

Bradamante, still gasping, turned to Merlin. "It worked."

Merlin inclined his head, his face lit by the glow of the crystal in his palm. "Excalibur exists in two worlds at once, this one and the spirit realm. The shade that animates a golem cannot be touched by mortal steel, for in this world it is incorporeal. But in the spirit realm, it may be struck. And Excalibur sent it straight back to Hell."

"That would have come in handy when we fought those demons at Saint-Julian's," Roland muttered.

Merlin arched a brow. "Demons, eh? They fear this sword."

Bradamante studied Excalibur in her hands. The weapon felt perfect in her grip, its weight balanced, its hilt molded to her hand as if she had been born to wield it. She was still marveling when Turpin called from the shadows.

"Over here. I think I've found your staff."

They hurried to him. The archbishop, rubbing his bruised shoulder, stood before the weapons rack they had seen in the Seeing Stone. The great spear still rested there, another blade beside it. But Turpin's eyes were fixed on the black staff, its carved runes gleaming in the crystal's glow.

"*Lorg Mór*," Merlin whispered, reverence in his voice. He reached out, and when his hands closed on the staff, he held it with a gentleness one might give a child.

Bradamante's gaze flicked from the chamber's

entrance, dim with the Lethe's glow, back to the wizard. "Now that you have it, what will we do?"

"First," he said, "I must undergo a brief transformation. Don't be alarmed, this is only a glamour. An illusion."

He gripped the staff in both hands and lifted its tip close to his face. Whispering a verse in that alien tongue, his form began to waver. His robes, his skin, his very features blurred and bent as though seen through water. In a heartbeat, Merlin was gone. Standing in his place was the young monk Eadric, handsome and whole, his gray robes replaced by a black Benedictine habit. The staff was nowhere to be seen.

"By God and good Saint Denis," Turpin breathed.

Roland's eyes widened. "What happened to the staff?"

"It's still with me," Eadric said, though his voice was Merlin's. "You simply can't see it."

Bradamante's jaw slackened. "She'll think Eadric has risen from the dead."

"That's the hope," Merlin replied. His borrowed face was solemn. "The illusion need not last long, just long enough for you to free Maugis."

"And then?" Roland pressed.

Merlin's lips tightened. "Then we fight like hell if we want any hope of leaving Avalon alive."

CHAPTER 29

LADY OF THE LAKE

Maugis' head throbbed as he hung, trapped within the web. The silver strands quivered with the skittering of the spiders. They were his jailors now, and they would remain so until Nimue chose to release him … unless she changed her mind and fed him to his keepers. He closed his eyes, numb from reliving the horrors of Verona, as what little hope he had left melted like ice.

The hinges of the iron-bound door creaked. He looked up, lids heavy, and saw her return at last. Still clad in her pale, gossamer dress, Nimue carried a black iron stand in one hand and cradled a vessel in the other. It was a cauldron, black as midnight, its belly adorned with a ram's head. Pearls, the color of bone, gleamed in the ram's eye sockets. Knotwork etched around the rim seemed to shift in the Lethe's glow, as though alive.

Maugis stifled a groan, his nerves burning with dread.

She set the stand before him and lowered the cauldron onto it. The ghost of a smile touched her lips.

"This is the Cauldron of Annwn," she said. "A window

into the darkest reaches of the Otherworld, and the realms beneath it. To look through that window, you must gaze into its fire."

Before he could draw his next breath, she sprinkled something into the cauldron. With a sudden roar, it erupted in flames. The scent of burning pitch filled his lungs as the fire blazed less than a yard from his face, the heat so fierce it nearly blistered his skin.

"Behold, Maugis, the pit of Hell." She bared her teeth. "Now look upon the souls you sent there."

His eyes grew wide. Within the flickering flames, he saw Angelica. Her face twisted into a silent scream as fire consumed her raven hair. Her eyes brimmed with panic as her skin blackened and blistered.

"No," he moaned, shutting his eyes, gritting his teeth. "I won't …"

"You will," Nimue said coldly, and snapped her fingers.

The spiders stirred. Needle-tips of their legs pressed against his cheeks. They slid beneath his eyelids and wrenched them open.

Angelica lay before him, her face little more than charred bone, yet her eyes remained wide, unblinking, filled with terror. The flames flared hotter; Maugis cried out at the sudden heat. Then, as the blaze subsided, she was gone.

Another lay in her place.

At once, Maugis knew him: every line of the face, though the jaw was harder, the features handsomer. His mind screamed the name.

Vivian.

His brother's long dark hair, the same he wore on the day Maugis killed him, now burned like Angelica's had. Flames licked between the rings of his mail as his sable cloak smoldered. Vivian's eyes held the same fear as Angelica's, but something deeper as well. A question. His lips moved soundlessly at first, then formed the words.

"Why ..."

Another breath. "Did you ..."

Maugis shuddered.

"Kill me ...?"

"I'm ... sorry," Maugis sobbed. "I didn't want ..." He could not finish the words.

Vivian's mouth opened wide in a scream, but no sound came. Instead, a torrent of fire poured out, consuming him, flesh and bone.

Then another figure lay in his place.

"No," Maugis huffed.

His father, Bevis, Count of Aygremont, burned in the flames. Fire wreathed the wolf-fur cloak he had worn the day of the hunt; his iron mail glowed like molten embers. His face was contorted with agony, his mouth twisted in a grimace. But his eyes, cold as ever, glared at Maugis with unyielding accusation.

"I didn't kill him," Maugis croaked.

Nimue narrowed her gaze. "Yet you were the reason he died. Orionde slew him so she could have you. You were the weapon that struck the mortal blow."

Maugis shook his head, the denial clawing in his throat. "No ... that's not true ... that's not what happened ..."

The charred skin peeled from his father's face, revealing white bone that blackened and cracked.

Maugis cried out, straining against the web. "God damn you—*stop!*"

BRADAMANTE FOLLOWED Roland and Merlin up the stairs that wound their way around the colossal tree. Turpin huffed behind her. She shifted her shoulder beneath the leather baldric Merlin had found beside the weapon rack, its strap stiff with age and decorated with interlaced ribbons. The baldric was fitted to a sturdy scabbard, its dark leather bound in delicate gold filigree, with the throat and chape gleaming with silver Celtic runes.

"The scabbard belonged to Arthur," Merlin had told her.

He must have been right, since Excalibur fit perfectly in the sheath, even though the baldric had been made for a man with much broader shoulders than hers. But for now, it would do.

As she climbed, Merlin's plan replayed in her mind. It would be a desperate gambit, but the only one they had.

Her heartbeat quickened as the stairs rose toward the terrace, towering a hundred feet above the Lethe. She glanced at the lake, with its moonlight glow, and remembered Maugis' warning: *The very name means oblivion. To drink its waters was to forget who you had ever been.*

Twenty feet from the terrace, her muscles tensed. She tried to steady her breath, as she always did before battle. Then her heart lurched at the sound of Maugis' scream.

"God damn you—*stop!*"

Bradamante tore Excalibur from its scabbard and bounded up the final steps.

IN ONE MOMENT, Maugis was screaming at Nimue. In the next, he stared in disbelief at a man he knew was dead.

The monk had emerged from the stairwell, his handsome face unblistered, his skin as fair as when Maugis first saw him upon entering Avalon.

Across the terrace, Nimue's eyes widened in disbelief. "Eadric?

"Nimue," the man whispered.

She shook her head. "How?"

The monk gave no reply as he reached out to embrace her. Then, before Maugis' eyes, Turpin eclipsed his view, brandishing his silver cross.

"By God and good Saint Denis," he bellowed, "begone!"

The spiders clinging to Maugis' head shrieked and released him, scurrying back up the web. Others fled into the branches as though terrified of the archbishop's holy fury. All but one, whose body exploded in a spray of black ichor as Durendal's blade split it in two.

Roland!

Another sword flashed, its hilt in Bradamante's hands. Its broad steel blade sheared through the web like linen threads. Maugis' gaze caught the round pommel and the gem set within it. "Is that ..."

"Excalibur," she said, cutting the strands near his wrist.

A shout drew his eyes back to the terrace. Nimue's arm was outstretched, her palm blazing with eldritch blue fire. The monk she had embraced was hurled backward, landing hard on his back. As he slid across the stone, the black habit melted away, and his face dissolved like water. Where Eadric had been, a stately figure in gray robes climbed to his feet, leaning on a black staff etched with runes. Beneath silver brows, his eyes burned like molten amber.

"Merlin ..." Nimue breathed, her voice trailing into silence, as if she truly had seen a ghost.

Maugis blinked. *Merlin?*

Nimue's voice rang out, the same verse that had paralyzed Maugis before. This time, she focused her power on the gray-robed man. Her right hand thrust forward, fingers spread wide, blue fire sparking at their tips. The fire raced toward the man's limbs, but it never struck. Instead, it flowed into the black staff, vanishing as though the wood itself drank it dry.

The man she'd called Merlin snapped the staff toward her, and the stolen fire jetted back out in a torrent. With a sound like a thunderclap, the blast struck Nimue and hurled her into the tree's stone-hard trunk.

The chittering of mandibles yanked Maugis' gaze to the web. Nimue's cry stirred the spiders into a frenzy, sending them swarming.

Turpin clutched his cross high. "Begone, I said!"

But the creatures no longer heeded him. One leapt at Roland, but he split it in midair with Durendal's steel. The rest rushed toward Maugis.

Bradamante cried out as she carved through the last strands binding his right wrist. Maugis tore his hand free and drew it to his lips, whispering into the crystal set into his ring.

"*Eoh!*"

Soul light lanced forth, bathing the spiders in its searing radiance. The arachnids recoiled and hissed, then scattered upward into the branches.

Bradamante slashed through more strands, freeing one of his legs. Roland caught Maugis by the shoulder, dragging him toward the terrace, while Excalibur's edge flashed and sliced the last silver threads that bound him.

His legs quivered as his feet touched solid ground for the first time in what felt like days. Cold weariness bled through his muscles.

"Here," Roland said, thrusting Maugis' staff into his hands. Maugis barely had time to clutch it before his gaze shot up in alarm at what was happening across the terrace.

Nimue rose into the air, arms outstretched, her toes dangling ten feet above the stone. Her gossamer dress whipped about her in an unseen wind, and her face was a mask of simmering rage.

"Enough, Nimue!" Merlin shouted.

He lowered his staff into the flames blazing in the Cauldron of Annwn. Fire leapt to the runes carved in its shaft, and with a sweep of his arm, he flung it toward her.

The fireball hurtled across the terrace. Nimue's hand flicked. The blaze twisted in midair and plunged over the parapet, exploding into the lake below.

"Guard!" she screamed.

The door to the terrace shuddered open. A sound of grinding hinges filled the air as an iron monstrosity stooped through the portal. The giant rose to its full height, ten feet tall, forged of black iron, its limbs joined by unnatural hinges. Its skull-like head swiveled toward Maugis and his companions, eyes burning with blue flame.

"What the hell is that?" Maugis muttered.

Roland grimaced. "A bloody golem." Then, gripping Durendal, he charged.

THE GOLEM SWEPT a massive hand toward Roland. He ducked and spun, the five iron fingers grazing the air above his head. Durendal crashed into the giant's knee, hard enough to crack the hinge, but not shear through.

Yet Roland was not alone.

With a cry, Bradamante charged from the other side. Excalibur sang as it struck, carving a gash into the golem's shin in a spray of sparks.

Black iron flashed. Roland raised his sword just in time

to catch the giant's clawing hand. The impact jarred his arms and sent him staggering back.

A fireball roared over his head, then a second. He glimpsed Maugis on the terrace, staff ablaze with the same fire that burned in the black cauldron. An explosion shook the stone, but Roland had no time to see what happened, for the iron golem lunged.

He darted aside as a huge finger scraped across the mail on his ribs. He spun and chopped at its wrist, but the blade struck only a glancing blow.

The blue fire in the golem's sockets flared with fury. Its backhand smashed into Roland's chest. The breath fled his lungs as his body hurtled backward. His skull cracked against the tree's trunk, and a storm of stars burst across his vision before all went black.

HOVERING ten feet above the terrace, flames licked at Nimue's tattered dress. Char streaked her cheeks, and ash dusted her slender limbs. With a flick of her wrist, she had hurled Merlin's fireball aside, but Maugis' followed, striking true and exploding in a burst of flame.

Yet still she hovered, and Maugis had never seen a woman more furious.

Her fingers curled into claws, wreathed in blue fire. Behind her, the colossal tree groaned as its stone-like bark split and splintered. With a savage thrust of her hands, a storm of jagged shards ripped free and hurtled toward them.

Merlin cried out as the shards struck like a swarm of hornets. Maugis flung his arms across his face and squeezed his eyes shut as the stony missiles shredded skin. Pain lanced through his chest and limbs.

When he opened his eyes, blood streaked his arms from dozens of cuts. Beside him, Merlin groaned. His gray robes hung in tatters, crimson seeping from the wounds beneath.

A crash of iron spun Maugis around. Bradamante gripped Excalibur with both hands, its blade gleaming after severing one of the iron giants' thighs in two. The crash was the rest of its leg striking the terrace. Then came a roar as Turpin threw all of his weight and strength into the giant's other leg. Without anything to balance on, the giant toppled. Bradamante darted aside as the massive body smashed through the parapet and plunged into the lake below with a resounding splash.

Maugis gaped at the six-foot gap in the shattered parapet, the stone crumbling into dust.

"You'll wish you hadn't done that," Nimue said coldly as she drifted back to the ground. Blue fire hissed along her fingertips. Her voice was calm, but her eyes blazed with fury.

"It took months to forge that golem. Yet it will take only seconds to end *your* life."

Her words sent a shiver down Maugis' skin.

Then Nimue's head turned. Her eyes narrowed past Merlin, confusion flickering across her face.

A thick violet fog billowed from the terrace stairs. It rolled across the stone, carrying the earthy scent of poppies, spreading toward them. Merlin glanced about, bewildered, but Maugis knew this mist. He had seen it before. At Rosefleur.

How is this possible?

The fog coiled around Nimue. For the first time, fear touched her gaze. She began to sway in the violet mist. She shook her head, as if trying to ward off its effects, but then her eyelids fluttered, her knees buckled, and she collapsed to the ground.

"What's happening?" Merlin asked hastily.

"It's a spell, it's put her into the Fae Sleep," Maugis replied, the full meaning of it dawning on him even as he spoke.

"A spell?" Merlin blinked. "Cast by whom?"

Before Maugis could answer, the flap of wings pulled Maugis' gaze to the railing. A raven swooped above the parapet and perched upon a bough twenty feet above. Its eyes burned with fire.

"Behold the Blackbird!" a man's voice called from the stairs.

Maugis' blood ran cold as it all began to make sense.

CHAPTER 30

THE BLACKBIRD

The thunder of boots pounding up the stairs shook the terrace.

Maugis and Merlin backed into the thinning violet mist, both clutching their staves, the tips still flickering with fire. Pain wracked Maugis' body with every breath, and he grimaced from the effort of standing.

Turpin dragged Roland toward them. The paladin moaned, rubbing the back of his skull, but his eyes were open. Bradamante glanced warily at the raven, then hurried to Maugis' side, Excalibur gleaming in her grip.

"You're bleeding," she said, her brow furrowed with worry.

"I know," Maugis said through clenched teeth.

The first man to emerge from the stairs was Ludgar, the mercenary captain whose life they had spared when they first landed in Britannia. Six hard-faced men followed, chainmail clinking, long swords at the ready. More poured after them, spreading across the far side of the terrace.

Next came a giant, at least seven feet tall, a bull of a man encased in chainmail, hefting a double-bladed axe.

His scarred face was as gray as a corpse, his eyes cold and dull. But it was the figure who stepped from the giant's shadow that stole Maugis' breath and sent his mind reeling.

Angelica.

Bradamante gasped, her knuckles whitening on Excalibur's hilt.

"How?" Maugis said, his voice raw. "I saw you fall into the fire …"

Her pale skin was unmarred by burns or scars, and her hair was pulled back, as dark as the close-fitting dress she wore. She was alive, and right then, she looked as terrifying and as beautiful as ever.

"Maugis," she said scornfully, "when you cast me into those burning stables, I discovered something about myself. I no longer needed a staff or a blade to wield power—only words, and my will. A gift from my mother, I suppose. When the flames closed around me, I willed them aside. When the floor collapsed and shattered my body, I willed bone and flesh to knit again. It took many nights before I was whole, but I emerged stronger than when you tried to destroy me."

Her gaze drifted upward, to the raven perched upon the bough. "And then I searched for my master. As you see, I found him."

Maugis gave the raven a sidelong glance. That black bird was not a bird at all, at least inside.

Bradamante's eyes grew wide with the same dreadful understanding. "Is that …?"

"Astaroth," Maugis whispered.

Merlin leaned close. "Who is she?"

"Morgain's daughter."

A mix of alarm and disbelief filled the wizard's eyes.

Then the giant spoke, in a voice Maugis knew all too

well—the same voice that had once come from Roland's lips.

"Maugis d'Aygremont," it said coldly, "I have waited many years to meet you again."

On the bough above, the raven's beak moved, and yet the words issued from the giant's corpse-gray mouth.

"You robbed me of my vessel," the giant continued, its voice rising, "the one that suited me best. And now you would rob me of the weapon? That blade belongs to me. Bring it here!"

Maugis' stomach coiled into a knot. "You can't do that," he told Bradamante under his breath.

"I know," she said.

"That sword," Merlin boomed, "belonged to Arthur, High King of Britain. You cannot have it."

The giant's eyes narrowed. "And who are you, old man, to speak to me so?"

"I am Merlin!"

At the name, Angelica's eyes widened.

"Perhaps you've heard of me," the wizard added.

"You are already dead," the giant said flatly. "All of you are, save for my old vessel. I will fill it again when the binding is broken with Aygremont's death. The weapon will feel good in his grip."

The giant turned, its corpse-like gaze fixing on the woman beside him.

"Angelica," it commanded, "destroy them!"

Angelica raised her arms, and the Cauldron of Annwn erupted in fire. Flames streaked skyward, then arced downward in a torrent aimed straight at Maugis.

His heart seized. He braced for the searing blast, but Merlin stepped in front of him, his rune-carved staff held high. The fire bent to the wood, sucked into it, and the runes blazed orange like molten steel. With a sweeping motion, Merlin unleashed the flames, sending a crescent of fire lashing across the terrace.

Screams filled the night. Half a dozen mercenaries writhed as the flames engulfed them, their hands clawing frantically at the fire.

"Kill them!" the giant roared.

And with that command, every mercenary still standing surged forward.

ROLAND REMEMBERED nothing of his demonic possession four years ago in Verona. All he knew was what his companions had told him. But one truth burned in him now: he would not let it happen again. So when the mercenaries surged, Roland sprang to his feet, Durendal in one hand and his dagger in the other, and charged.

Ludgar was the first to meet him. Their swords clashed, but Roland's strength broke the man's guard. Durendal punched through Ludgar's mail and deep into his gut. Shock glazed the mercenary's eyes as Roland ripped the blade free and spun to meet the next man.

He parried one blow, then another, before driving his dagger into the man's armpit. He forced it in until he felt the heart give way. To his left, Turpin bellowed a battle cry and brought his flanged mace down on a mercenary's skull. Bone crunched; the man dropped lifeless.

A jet of fire roared overhead. Roland ducked, then sprang back as a severed head rolled past his boots. Bradamante stood to his right, Excalibur gleaming in her hands, a headless body crumpled at her feet.

"Can you handle the rest?" she asked before parrying another mercenary's blow.

"Yes," Roland said through gritted teeth as he rammed

Durendal between the cheekplates of a mercenary's helmet.

"Good," she said, right before Excalibur took off her opponent's arm.

She fell back.

Then Roland and Turpin pressed forward deeper into the fray.

~

BRADAMANTE PRAYED that Roland and Turpin could hold their ground as she scanned the chaos of the terrace.

Mercenaries still aflame hurled themselves screaming over the parapet into the Lethe, plunging more than a hundred feet to oblivion. The rest had formed a crescent of steel in front of the giant and Angelica, trading blows with Roland and Turpin. Merlin, meanwhile, was locked in a fiery duel with Angelica. She drew flame from the cauldron and hurled it at him; he absorbed it into his staff and flung it back, only for her to swat it aside with some invisible force wielded by a flick of her hand.

That left Maugis.

He stood a yard behind Merlin, staff raised as if ready to fend off another fireball. But his face betrayed him, twisted with pain. Bleeding cuts scored his arms, his legs through torn breeches, and across his chest where his tunic had ripped to tatters. She knew his ailment meant those wounds would not clot. His magic might heal him, but not in the midst of this battle. He was bleeding out before her eyes. They had to end this now.

And she knew how.

She hurried to his side, raising Excalibur. "This blade can harm Astaroth. Merlin said it exists in two worlds at the same time, this one and the spirit realm."

Maugis nodded, comprehension flickering in his eyes. Then his gaze darted to the raven. It perched twenty feet above, hopping along the branch, its beak clacking while its words poured from the giant's mouth.

"Kill them! Kill them all!"

Maugis grimaced. "How can you possibly reach him?"

"I can if you move him." She pointed at the hulking giant. "Cast his spirit into that empty vessel. And I'll finish it."

Maugis stared at her. "You're brilliant."

"I know," she said, and pulled him close, pressing her lips to his.

Their eyes locked for a second, then she pulled away. "Let's end this."

As the din of battle raged around—roaring fire, clashing steel, men screaming, and men dying—Maugis closed his eyes, remembering the verse he spoke that day atop the tower in Verona. Once it was etched in his mind, he let go of his staff. It clattered onto the stone floor. He took a step back and focused his gaze on the raven.

"Astaroth!" Maugis cried.

The raven craned its neck at the sound of its name.

With the demon's true name spoken, Maugis began reciting the verse, the words of power falling from his tongue with the cadence of a requiem.

"No!" the giant roared from across the terrace. "Stop him!"

Eldritch blue fire wreathed the raven's feathers, its eyes wide with terror.

"Astaroth, spawn of Samyaza, by the power of the Fae

and the angels, your masters in heaven, I bind you—" Maugis pointed at the corpse-gray giant. "Into that!"

The raven let out a shriek.

The demon's spirit tore from the bird's body and streaked toward the giant like a bolt of lightning. It struck the giant with a flash of blue fire. The axe fell from the monster's fingers as it staggered backward.

Bradamante sprinted toward the giant through a gap in the mercenary line carved by Roland's blade, and then she leaped into the air, raising Excalibur high above her head.

"For Roland!" she cried as she brought the sword down with two hands. Its tip landed in the giant's gaping mouth, shearing through his jaw, then continuing down his neck and into his chest. Violet fire exploded from the wound, and for an instant, Maugis could see the faint outline of Astaroth's form clinging to the giant's flesh.

A roar like a man facing the fires of Hell burst from the giant's throat.

The violet blaze hissed into smoke. Bradamante wrenched Excalibur free as the giant toppled backward and crashed onto the flagstones.

Angelica screamed.

Then, with a thunderous roar, the Cauldron of Annwn exploded. And before Maugis' eyes, everything vanished behind a wave of fire and smoke.

CHAPTER 31

OBLIVION

In the thinning smoke, bodies littered the terrace. A shudder ran through Maugis. Bradamante lay closest, Excalibur a yard from her limp hand, her auburn hair singed, her face streaked with soot. He dropped to his knees and gathered her in his arms.

Her breath warmed his cheek. *She's alive …*

Relief flooded him as her chest rose and fell with a steady rhythm. Within him, a glimmer of hope swelled.

Until he heard his name.

"Maugis …"

Angelica emerged from the fading smoke, her face stricken with grief. She stumbled toward him, eyes staring through him as if into a void. "Why?" she pleaded. "Why did you take him from me?"

Maugis rose to his feet. "That book made you his slave. But you're free now. You have no master."

A tear slid down her soot-stained cheek. "I was never his slave."

Her sleeves hung in tatters, revealing dark red symbols branded along her right arm. They were the price she had paid, the remnants of the ward she defeated to claim the *Book of Shadows.*

"But you were," Maugis said softly. "That's what he does. He twists, he uses. Verona, Roland, even this. None of it was you. It was him."

Her mouth fell open, sorrow deep in her eyes. "Do you mean that?"

"Yes."

She stepped closer, wrapped her arms around him, and sobbed against his shoulder. Then her lips found his, wet with salt tears. She kissed him again, this time with the passion they had shared as lovers.

He kissed her back. First her lips, then her throat.

Her hand caressed the back of his neck and moved to his hair. His locks slipped through her fingers. Then she closed them, tightening her grip, and pulled.

Her eyes flashed with fury. "I want you to bring him back!"

Maugis' stomach clenched; pain seared from the back of his head.

"Bring him back!" she screamed. She tore at his hair, trying to rip it from his scalp.

In that moment, he knew she was lost. Yet maybe there was still one way to save her …

Ignoring the pain as she tugged at his hair, he gathered her in his arms and staggered toward the shattered parapet.

"I won't bring him back," he grimaced.

"You will!" she hissed. "Or I will torture you." Her eyes drifted to Bradamante lying unconscious on the terrace. "And I will torture *her* until you have no choice but to return him to me!"

"I can save you instead," he cried as she pulled harder on his hair. He glanced sideways. They stood three feet from the remnants of the parapet, with the waters of the Lethe a hundred feet below.

She wrenched his head back, her green eyes simmering as she bore into his. "I don't need to be saved—I need *him!*"

"No, you don't."

Summoning all of his strength, Maugis threw her off him. Her fingers tore free of his hair, taking a fistful of bloodied locks still wrapped in her fingers. Then he lunged and pushed her over the ledge.

Angelica's scream echoed through Avalon as she plunged a hundred feet into the Lethe.

Maugis darted for the stairs. He flew down them, four at a time, barely keeping his balance as he went. When he reached the bottom, he hurdled over the hulking tree roots and spotted the boat. He glanced at the lake. Thirty yards away, Angelica was flailing in the glowing waters.

He jumped in the boat and rowed as fast as he could. When he reached her, she clutched desperately for the hull. He grabbed her wrists and pulled her inside.

She looked up at him, wet raven hair slick across her forehead. Her green eyes were wide and wondering, as innocent as a child's.

"Thank … you," she huffed between breaths.

She blinked water from her eyes. "Who are you?"

Maugis managed a weary smile, knowing his plan had worked. The Lethe means "Oblivion." There could not have been a more extreme yet necessary cure. She would not know herself, or him, or the love they shared. But most of all, she would not remember Astaroth. Or the *Book of Shadows.* Or the poison he placed in her mind.

"I'm someone who loves you," he whispered.

Her lips parted. "Oh …"

"Now let's get you to shore."

MAUGIS LEFT Angelica by the boat and hurried back to the stairs. Halfway up, weakness seized him. His muscles throbbed, his head swam. In his rush to save Angelica, he had forgotten his own wounds. The cuts still bled, dozens of them, and would not close on their own. But his friends were up there. Bradamante had survived, but what of Turpin and Roland?

He braced himself against the titanic trunk, forcing his legs to climb. By the time he neared the top, he was crawling, his vision blurring as though the Lethe itself had seeped into his veins. He touched a hand to the terrace floor, his vision fading. And then—

Soul light.

Its glow warmed his skin, banishing the weariness that had consumed him just moments ago. He was sitting, propped up against the wall with Merlin kneeling before him, a crystal filled with a familiar pearlescent glow pinched between his thumb and forefinger.

Bradamante knelt beside him, hope shining in her eyes. He felt her hand in his. Over Merlin's shoulder, Turpin and Roland looked on. All four of them were soot-stained with singed hair and a reek of smoke. But they were alive. Whatever Angelica had done to the Cauldron of Annwn, the blast must have been more flash than fire. The Cauldron itself had split in two, its jagged halves lying several yards apart. The bodies of mercenaries sprawled across the terrace, but the corpses bore wounds from battle. They had died fighting his friends.

"That should do it," Merlin said. The light in his crystal dimmed, and he tucked it into a pocket of his tattered robes. "How do you feel?"

"Better than I did," Maugis admitted.

Merlin offered his hand and pulled him to his feet. Bradamante wrapped her arms around him.

"You gave us quite a scare," she whispered.

"So did you," Maugis replied. "When the Cauldron exploded, I feared I'd lost you. All of you."

"By God and Saint Denis," Turpin said with a grin, "death passed us by this day."

Roland clapped the archbishop on the shoulder. "That it did," he said. "After all, we still have a prophecy to fulfill."

Maugis glanced at Bradamante's hip, where Excalibur rested in its scabbard, and cocked his head. "What do you mean?" he asked. "We have the weapon. What more is there to do?"

"I believe your friend Roland is speaking of my prophecy," Merlin said. "A vision that came to me in my cave of dreams. I call it the prophecy of the once and future king."

Maugis glanced at the others. Judging by their expressions, they had heard this tale before.

Merlin spread his hands. "The legends say Arthur will come again when the land needs him most. So I believed, until I met your friends. When I beheld these two," he gestured to Roland and Turpin, "I knew their faces: Lancelot, the king's finest warrior, and Cadoc, his trusted counsellor. And the more I look at the Lady Bradamante, I see echoes of Galahad from a time long past. And then, I saw you. The resemblance is less striking, but when I watched you wield the power …"

His eyes fixed on Maugis, burning with certainty. "I knew a man like you once. That man was me."

Maugis drew in a breath, the weight of Merlin's words settling over him.

"So, this future king was never Arthur," Merlin said.

"Your friends tell me his name is Charles. And he has you, his paladins, to sit at his own table. He is the king your age needs, one to forge the kingdom that eluded Arthur. The one to bring light into the darkness."

As he listened, Maugis felt a chill of recognition. "Orionde spoke of the same vision. A new empire to save Europe from darkness."

"All we have to do," Bradamante said with a faint smile, "is help make it happen."

Merlin cleared his throat. "We should go." He glanced at Nimue, still lying where the Fae Sleep had claimed her. "We had best be gone from Avalon before she wakes."

THEY LEFT Glastonbury the next morning. Turpin spent a handful of silver coins to procure five horses for the road to Hamwick, the fishing village they had passed after crossing the Channel. Each paladin rode their own. Maugis chose a piebald gelding and sat comfortably in the saddle, reins in one hand, his book satchel slung over his shoulder.

Dressed in a new tunic and riding cloak, Merlin rode with Angelica behind him. Before they had left, Maugis had asked Merlin to take her to the grotto near Verona.

"I swore an oath to Morgain that I would save her daughter," Maugis had told him. "I need you to help me keep it."

The wizard was more than willing to oblige. "I would very much like to see Morgain again," he had said. "We were close once, in Avalon. And besides, after nearly three hundred years, she might be the only friend I have left."

The wizard looked content as they rode away from Glastonbury toward the ruins of Camelot, perched on a distant hill. Angelica clung to him, her head turning to take in the countryside, eyes wide and bright as though seeing the world's beauty for the first time.

Maugis smiled, then looked away. She was his past, but would not be his future.

He turned to Bradamante, riding beside him on a dun-colored mare. Even with singed hair, she was beautiful. But she was so much more than that. Brave beyond measure, and brilliant. Without her waking Merlin and figuring out how to stop Astaroth, they and their mission would have been doomed. He would forever be in her debt. And she had already suggested a few ways he might repay it.

His gaze drifted to Excalibur, its hilt bouncing above her hip. The gemstone set into its round pommel gleamed in the sunlight.

They had done it. Orionde's mission was fulfilled.

But a greater task remained: the empire still to be forged, with countless battles still to be won. For the rest of his days, *that* would be his mission.

For Charles, and for Francia.

HISTORICAL NOTE

Of all my novellas, *Merlin Reborn* was my favorite to write. I am a fan of history and fantasy, and this one has plenty of both.

In 773, Charlemagne marched his army across the Alps into Italy after his brother Carloman's sudden death left him sole ruler of the Franks. Carloman's young widow, Gerberga, fled with her sons to the Lombard king Desiderius, who placed them in the care of his son, Adalgis, in Verona. Meanwhile, Desiderius threatened Rome itself, which led the Pope to call upon Charlemagne for aid.

By September, Charles had besieged the Lombard capital of Pavia, while a smaller force surrounded Verona. From here, my tale leaves history for fantasy. In truth, Verona's siege was brief and bloodless: Adalgis slipped away to Constantinople, Gerberga and her sons surrendered, and the city opened its gates to Charles. Only Pavia resisted, until its fall in 774 ended the Lombard kingdom.

The love affair between Gerberga and Adalgis, the climbing of Verona's walls, and the darker forces at work within them are all my creation.

Within this historical context, I reimagined the central narrative by adapting one of the most famous Renaissance tales about Charlemagne's paladins: *Orlando Furioso*, by Ludovico Ariosto. In that epic poem, Orlando (Roland), Charlemagne's greatest paladin, descends into madness after discovering that his beloved, the beautiful pagan princess Angelica, has eloped with a Moorish soldier. Heartbroken and betrayed, Orlando loses his wits in a fit of jealous fury and wanders the world in savage madness, leaving destruction in his wake.

It seemed natural to recast Roland's madness as the result of demonic possession, and Astaroth proved a perfect fit. He is one of the few named demons to appear in the medieval legends collectively known as the *Matter of France*, and he's often connected to Maugis d'Aygremont. Although Maugis does not appear in *Orlando Furioso*, he is a frequent figure in the Carolingian cycle and plays a role akin to Merlin in Arthurian myth.

In the Historical Note for *The Sorceress of Avalon*, I explained how the legends of Charlemagne eventually became entangled with characters from the stories of King Arthur, especially Merlin and Morgana le Fay (Morgain in my novellas). These novellas gave me my first (and so far only) opportunity to write about two of the most iconic figures from Arthurian mythology. But the more I explored their stories, the more I felt drawn to imagine Arthur himself, along with Lancelot and the other knights of the Round Table. From that impulse came the scene in the Crystal Cave, which depicts the legendary Battle of Camlann.

The title of T.H. White's classic *The Once and Future King* inspired Merlin's prophecy in my story. My twist—that the "future king" would be Charlemagne rather than Arthur—felt natural, given the deep parallels between the two legendary traditions. Many of Charlemagne's paladins share qualities with the knights of the Round Table, and in the medieval and Renaissance tales, Roland and Lancelot are often two faces of the same hero.

Finally, I owe a debt of gratitude to the great authors who have reimagined the Arthurian legends over the years. These include Mary Stewart and her *Merlin Trilogy*, Bernard Cornwell and his *Warlord Chronicles*, and, more recently, Giles Kristian and his powerful trilogy: *Lancelot*, *Camelot*, and *Arthur*. I highly recommend them all. As a small homage to these writers, I titled several chapters in Part Three after their books.

This may be the end of Maugis' tale, but for two monks at the monastery of Derry, and a young widow in the heart of Aquitaine, the story is only just beginning.

The story continues in *Enoch's Device*, where the *Dragon-Myth Cycle* begins.

About the Author

Joseph Finley writes historical fantasy that mixes medieval history, myth, and a dash of magic. He's a longtime fan of knights, old legends, classic fantasy paperbacks, and wandering through castles and cathedrals on his travels. Most evenings you'll find him with a glass of wine in hand, and most mornings he's back at it, surrounded by history books and chasing down the next story.

To receive a **free short story**, as well as updates on Joseph's next novel and special offers, join his Reader List by signing up **here** or at his website, below:

www.authorjosephfinley.com

Lastly, if you enjoyed this book, please consider leaving a review (even if it's only a line or two) at Amazon or Goodreads. Word-of-mouth is essential to an author's success, so your input is greatly appreciated!

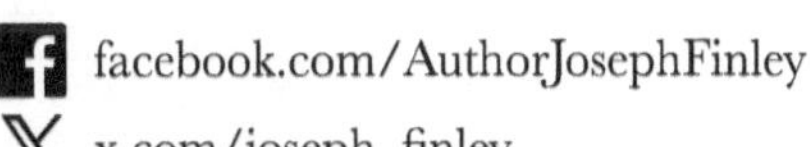

facebook.com/AuthorJosephFinley

x.com/joseph_finley

instagram.com/josephfinley

www.ingramcontent.com/pod-product-compliance
Lightning Source LLC
Chambersburg PA
CBHW032015050726
47590CB00006B/2183